Nudist Adventures Collection

Max Goo

Published by Max Goo, 2023.

NUDIST ADVENTURES COLLECTION

First edition. January 25, 2023.

ISBN: 979-8215384190

Written by Max Goo.

Author's note: All characters depicted in this work of fiction are 18 years of age or older.
The characters are adults, and the activities entirely consensual.

Follow Max Goo in all the usual places to get a notification the next time I publish a naughty story for your delight.

BOOK ONE

First Time Cuckold

The location for my first accidental cuckold experience was a so-called sun club, which was a house transformed into a nudist venue.

If you have been there you might know it from a brief description: the house had been altered and adapted to offer extended wet facilities; I'm talking jacuzzis, sauna, and steam rooms.

The cafe area was in what anyone else might call the knocked-through, open-plan living room. There were various "relaxing" rooms, with or without locks on the doors, and a surprisingly tiny minuscule garden for a place that has the word "sun" in its description.

We were at this venue, and it was one of those places where men outnumbered women by a ratio of about twenty to one.

My wife was getting plenty of admiring looks, and I was intrigued to realize that I wasn't jealous. I rather enjoyed the compliment; I enjoyed showing off my beautiful wife and her alluring body.

We attracted a crowd, or at least she had crowds of followers, wherever we went. In the shower, in the jacuzzi, in the shower, in the steam room, in the shower, in the sauna, and back in the shower.

Yes, we kept showering!

It was hot and tiring.

If you've ever done it, you will know that all that heat is draining. So then we went to investigate the relaxation rooms, where we discovered a whole other world.

We were just hoping to cool down, but we quickly found out about the other activities that went on behind those closed doors.

The doors weren't always closed, for one thing.

Leaving them ajar was a trend, whether to let in cooler air or just accommodate the voyeurs, I'm not sure.

The rooms were already occupied, every single one, with one or two men inside.

Yes, the occupants may have been relaxing, but they were looking around and alert, and it seemed they were waiting for something to happen.

And that something appeared to be Melissa (or any other female). Men beckoned us into their rooms, but we ignored the gesturing as we explored.

Another man helpfully whispered to us, explaining that we only had to ask, and anyone would give up a room for us, whichever room we wanted. The magic key to any room was Melissa, my hot wife.

In this particular part of the building, just about every man had his towel wrapped around his nether regions, like a skirt. There were even a variety of ways in which to wear your towel.

The trendier guys with the best physiques, to show off, had folded their towels in half, lengthways, which resulted in very skimpy short skirts atop long muscular legs.

The more mature men, with a little extra padding, wore towels in a more conventional style, resulting in a long skirt that went from somewhere around their midriff to almost reaching their knees.

I'm embarrassed to say that I wasn't up on the latest in toweling fashions at that time.

But so much for nudism; why were they not happy to go naked?

Earlier in the day, my wife and I had already identified the most attractive-looking men, those she'd most like to be locked in a room with. The men had been less bashful, leaving towels all abandoned.

In the steam room and the sauna men sat in the way that men usually sit; with legs spread and knees wide apart, they took up as much space as possible with the meat and potatoes on full display. Some had erections, some did not, and some even touched themselves: some were subtle, and others overt.

I would say in your face, but not literally, I don't want you to get the wrong idea.

I had certainly noted the faces of the men who supported the pythons.

I didn't know what was going to happen, but if it were to happen, I'd like to see my wife with one of those. I later found out she'd had much the same thoughts.

She looked at me, I looked at her, and we did that silent communicating thing that you can do with your best friend and soulmate. We turned around and went to the first room where a man was "relaxing" by lying down leaving it all on display, and with his knob in hand.

Relaxing?

How could he be relaxing with troops of people walking past his open door?

Not just the door, but his eyes were open too. He knew what was going on. My wife had spotted him earlier, and so had I. We'd both noted his mega cock barely hidden by his towel-skirt.

I certainly wondered how big that trouser snake would get when fully hard.

With his assets, he could afford to lie there and just wait for the action to come to him.

Lucky bugger.

Of course, he wasn't just a big walking dick; he had other things going for him too. I'd guess he was in his thirties with a reasonably fit body. Perhaps he went to the gym, swam regularly, or just had an active job; he wasn't ripped like a magazine model but fit-looking.

Attractive with a gentle face, blond hair, and blue eyes.

Is that a bit weird, noticing another man's eyes? Let me tell you, they were so blue you couldn't not notice them; tinted contact lenses probably.

"May we come in and join you?" Melissa asked. She may be tiny, but she's courageous.

He instantly sat up and swung his legs around to get off the relaxation couch. Like a gentleman, he stood as she entered the room.

I invited in two of the men behind us, there was something about them, more fit bodies, and I thought they'd add to the party atmosphere in the room. They walked in, past me, and I lagged behind, where I turned to shut the door and lock it.

When I turned around, I was delighted to see my wife was totally in her element, as she had been all day. So there were three men, plus myself and my wife in this room, which suddenly didn't feel like it was big enough. Melissa was in the midst of it all and had climbed onto the bed.

I'm calling it a bed for want of a better name; I don't know what you'd call it.

Not a massage couch, it was too sturdy and robust to be that. It was a permanent, fixed table constructed in the middle of the room, with a padded top covered in black leather or leather-like material. Easy to clean.

Melissa was on the table on her knees, surrounded by the three men.

They had all dropped their towels, and she seemed to be examining the goods on offer. By examining, I mean only looking; the touching didn't begin immediately.

She was on her knees with her legs slightly apart, which looked fantastic, by the way, with her hands on her breasts. Underneath them, to be more precise, holding them up as if presenting them to the men. I imagined her offering her breasts in return for what they could give her.

I had been supporting a semi for much of the day, but now it was as stiff as a broom handle. The towel was getting in the way, so I released it, letting it drop to the floor. Still standing by the door, I gripped my tool and tugged it gently.

The other men were all just as hard and had the same idea as me regarding modestly covering up or the lack thereof.

Towels abandoned; these naked men were looking at my wife with a mixture of hungry desire and admiration.

At that moment, I felt proud of her for putting on a fantastic display that would only get better and far more filthy. And proud of myself for getting such a hot woman to marry me.

And proud of myself for bringing such an up-for-it woman to a place like this.

I felt like a rock star.

No matter what these blokes did with her, no matter what she did to them, I'd brought her here, and I would take her home. You could say she'd come on my arm, but don't take it too literally.

As I remained by the door, watching my wife surrounded by three buck-naked men with dicks pointing to the ceiling, I remained proud and eager to watch, come what may.

I'd like to watch my wife getting off on these men.

See her touching their toned bodies and sucking their cocks, all three of them.

Watch her getting fucked by them.

Could she take all three at once? One in her mouth, one in her ass, and one in her cunt? Probably not, not if she was going to enjoy it; this was real life, not a fucking porn-test-of-endurance show.

Could I somehow telepathically tell my wife what I wanted?

We hadn't talked about it.

But at that second, I saw the appeal in watching my wife with the men.

At that point, I was still planning to take part.

I thought I might lead the assault, be the start of the show with these three as our audience, come in at the end to claim her final orgasm, or be right in the middle directing all the action.

I was still at the door when they started to touch her.

Blue-eyes started tentatively at first, but as his advances were welcomed, the others grew increasingly bolder.

She certainly looked like she'd be making a show of herself with the strangers, and I damn well knew the men would all be up for it.

Can you imagine in that situation saying to the guys how do you feel about fucking my wife? Who wouldn't say yes?

And then you present them an option; you say, you can either fuck my wife in her incredible, tight pussy, or let her suck your cock until you come in her mouth, over her face, or over those jiggling jugs. Or, if you're not into that kind of thing, you can leave.

Not that it was a certainty that the men would be invited to fuck my wife.

She was my wife, after all. I think they'd have been pretty pleased if they could have watched me fuck her, and even more so if there was a little hand relief to go around; anything else was a big bonus.

Big Bonus Time.

No one asked the men what they wanted; we assumed they would be up for it.

I looked at Melissa; she looked at me, she looked down at my cock in my hand, and I nodded.

"You've got a choice here; which one are you going to suck first?"

The biggest grin broke across her face, like a kid in a sweet shop.

It was as if someone had offered that kid as many of whichever sweets she wanted. I don't know what the men thought, but if I'd been one of them and heard the husband say that, I'd be pretty excited.

This was not the time to be shy.

We'd already tossed aside our towels so my girl could make a choice, a considered and informed choice, based on a close inspection of the goods on offer.

Her nipples were hard.

There was a man on either side of her.

Blue Eyes, and another had their hands on her breasts, stroking, caressing, holding her melons. Holding her big wobbly tits in their hands and squeezing.

The look of delight on her face was rewarding, squirming while trying to keep it together, trying to hold on to her dignity and self-control as she melted like putty in their hands.

The men didn't know it, but she was prepared to do anything for them. They only had to ask.

I can only guess how much her pussy might have been dripping as the third man moved in with his fingers. I watched his left hand disappear between her thighs.

"Oh," she let out a soft moan.

Melissa took a cock in each hand and bent forwards to take the third one in her mouth. She sucked it in greedily.

"Nice," one of the men murmured, "very nice."

Indeed was very nice to watch, like my very own porno movie going on right before my eyes. Melissa groaned and moaned, squirming with pleasure.

Maybe these three were too much for her to handle.

While one man caressed her breasts gently, I could see the other had run his fingers down to her nipple, giving it a gentle pull. He then rolled it between his fingers, and I imagined how much her pussy must've gushed with joy juice, having done that to her before myself.

Still, with two cocks in hand, she let the dick drop from her mouth and lifted her head to look between all three men, ignoring me entirely.

With her tongue out, she moved between the three of them, licking them over, lapping like a dog, teasing the men, and sucking up every pearl of pre-cum. Darting from one to the other, not lingering to focus on any one of them for long enough.

I moved my fingers over the end of my cock, wiping the slippery precum around the crown, mimicking what I saw her doing to them.

She was licking just enough to be felt, just enough to tease, but not enough to relieve the ache that I knew must be building up in their balls.

That's my wife, a real tease.

It was difficult to know which things she was enjoying most when there was a man fingering her, two men touching her boobs, touching three cocks available close-up, or the fact her husband was watching.

My balls ached, and my dick was as hard as ever; I pulled on the skin and rubbed it.

Despite knowing I was there, Melissa never gave me a second glance after making that first eye contact, that first unspoken agreement that this was what we would do.

She directed the scene, the men for her willing accomplices I wasn't invited to join in.

It dawned on me that there was a reason Melissa was teasing their cocks with the end of her tongue and not sucking any one of them in deeply into her mouth, and I know she does like sucking dick. There had to be a reason she wasn't doing it.

She needed to moan and groan.

The event was so exciting for her, and whatever the guy did with his fingers in her pussy was all too much. She couldn't clamp her lips around any one of those members because she was too turned on.

"Has anyone got any condoms?" she asked.

We hadn't planned this, but fortunately, we were the only ones unprepared. The other guys were prepared and optimistic.

It seemed every man had a condom. They all responded positively to the question, and the two men holding her breasts let go and reached for the little bags they had been carrying. The man with his fingers in her was more considerate and didn't withdraw.

Between them, the men seemed to come to some unspoken agreement about who was going first (without consulting me).

One of them got a condom out of the packet, tossed the packet on the floor, and slipped the condom over his hard dick — the others stepped back to watch.

Mr. Fingers continued doing the fingering.

With two men out of the way, my wife bent over and gobbled the cock of Mr. Fingers, and she sucked him deep inside. Not quite a deep throat, but doing her best.

He was a big boy. I'm not surprised that she couldn't fit him all in. My wife is no deep throat specialist, but she does a great job and what she does with her tongue more than makes up for what she lacks in opening up her own throat.

When she released the cork from her mouth, she said," Let me shuffle to the end of this bed and suck while this guy fucks me."

Fingers was to get his cock sucked, at the same time as the first guy with the condom was to give it to her from behind. This left Blue-Eyes and me on the outside.

From the outside, it was unclear exactly who came first but knowing her as I do, I'm pretty sure it was all too much for Melissa.

Soon she was jerking uncontrollably, and the guys stood little chance. Fingers withdrew, probably for safety; you wouldn't want your member too near those teeth when she was so out of control, or did she spit it out? The man at the rear, without a nickname, didn't get away in time. He held onto her hips so she could not slip away and thrust in and out hard. When her screams indicated she was coming, his grunts suggested he did too.

Barely missing a beat, Blue-Eyes ripped open his packet, put the latex jacket on, and was ready to take his place as an opening became available.

Remember I told you he had an impressive package; this proved to be correct.

We'd picked three excellent, well-hung studs for this activity.

Should that be the credit to them or create us for choosing well? Whatever.

Blue-Eyes was big, the sort of man who could give others an inferiority complex.

Having already been taken to the dizzying heights of some new plateau, Melissa was wet and ready for him. He was just what she wanted at that moment, I would guess. Watching that long thick dick disappear inside her was something to behold.

All of us watched in fascination, and the other two men moved in close. Between them, they stroked her back and hair.

I was still by the door, still single-handedly tackling my todger.

Amidst the moans, groans, and panting, there were real words. "Oh yes. That's big. Give it to me." Melissa obviously felt this big guy needed a few directions. "Slow. Faster. More!"

Very soon, she was coming again; that was obvious. Blue-Eyes, however, had more self-restraint and other things in mind. She collapsed on the table, arms too weak to hold her body up.

Blue-Eyes leaned over her and whispered something, then with his help, she turned around so that she was lying on her back. He began to thrust again, still standing and now with a clear view of her body and easy reach to rest his hand on her clit.

The other two men ensured her whole body was getting attention.

This time, in this position Blue-Eyes' python, did spit its load.

This left only Fingers and me as yet to be satisfied.

Perhaps more than anyone, Mr. Fingers had most enjoyed Melissa's shaven haven that day.

I know how heavenly it can feel sliding fingers around that soft, hairless skin and dipping into the wet folds. Just touching it, that area, when it is completely freshly shaved, is a fantastic experience in itself.

It looks nice, it feels nice, and it tastes nice.

Her reaction to the foreplay was predictable.

After touching and exploring it for so long, Mr. Fingers wanted in.

Without acknowledging me, he grabbed his handy condom.

Melissa was still lying down; there had been no time for recovery. But Mr. Fingers pulled her up to a sitting position at the very end of the bed. He held his cock, positioned it at her wet entrance, and eased it in.

Until this point, it had not registered in my mind that Mr. Fingers appendage was easily as big as the python, if not a little larger. If your tool is that size, you know any woman will need plenty of build-up before admission.

Melissa was worked up and ready.

Fingers had a different approach to offer; when he was fully inside, he held her tight to him, and she put her arms around his shoulders, clinging onto him. Then he stood up, taking all her weight in his arms and around his cock.

In this position, with gravity pulling her down, Melissa was helpless, whereas Fingers was in control of their pleasure. He used her like a doll drawing her up and down over him.

Redundant, the rest of us watched (somewhat impressed by his strength and technique). Of course, I can do that same position too, but for how long? There is always the risk of falling over.

For all the impressiveness of this maneuver, it didn't last long. Mr. Fingers carefully placed the exhausted lady back down on the table. He withdrew his cock, then kissed her gently on the cheek before picking up his towel and dealing with the condom.

Melissa looked sated.

Both of my two hands were working my dick, pulling the full length with one and cradling the crown with the other.

I came. In the palm of my hand

At that point, I experienced a revelation, my epiphany. I didn't need to join in. I enjoyed watching her enjoy what was on offer.

She tasted the rare delicacy of other men instead of feeding on the same meal she gets all the time (me).

I wanted each one of them to make her come.

And then I wanted to see them come with her, in her cunt or mouth or covering her enormous wobbling round breasts.

BOOK TWO

Cuckold in the Merry Meadow

There's no better way of spending a Tuesday afternoon than having sex with at least two men or preferably more. When most people are in the office and kids are at school every woman should treat herself to a bunch of horny naked men.

I prefer to start the week wedged between two strangers – men I've never met before – while my husband keeps an eye on proceedings. Imagine anonymous men politely standing in line, waiting their turn to find pleasure in one of my holes.

Unfortunately, I don't do that thing every day, not weekly. We look forward to our midweek daytime adventures as a treat, and we visit adult-only nudist and swingers venues to find willing participants.

My husband likes the couple's events because he's into women, but luckily he also likes to treat me to a bit of what I fancy.

I fancy *men* (mostly)

and *lots* of them.

I'm a greedy girl.

Midweek is when the male members massively outnumber the women in attendance.

Men don't mind turning up alone.

I wouldn't say women never attend naturist clubs on their own, but it's rare. I can't imagine going alone, but I don't need to because my husband is more than willing to let me have fun.

In the summer months, we like to go to enjoy the great outdoors without clothes, but if we get our hopes up for something specific, you can bet a freak weather front will bring in a bitter, biting wind, with side helpings of rain and hail.

We always take a *no-pressure, "see what happens"* attitude to our adventures. I don't recommend starting out with a preconceived notion of how things should develop; you can be sure they won't go that way.

Instead, we have no expectations, and if nothing happens, we will still have a nice relaxing time together.

Nevertheless, some of our day trips have turned into sexy erotic escapades.

At an adult-only space where there are many naked men and just a handful of naked women, the odds stack up rather nicely in my favor, and it doesn't take much to get the sort of session I crave.

ONE OF MY FAVORITE sessions took place in The Meadow. It was a Thursday lunchtime and involved a bunch of men who'd come along on their own, a field, and me.

I wasn't on my own; of course, my husband was with me. He watched and directed some of the action. Judging by the number of times he's mentioned it since it must be one of his favorite memories too.

Everyone in The Meadow had to enter that big gate and pay an entrance fee. Nudism was expected, swinging was commonplace, and there was no danger of offending anyone. Those things make me feel safe, and I need to feel safe to do the sort of stuff that I did that day.

MARCUS, MY HUSBAND, has some excellent sunglasses. I disliked them until I learned to appreciate their benefits for communal nude sunbathing, so I bought the same for myself.

I like to see someone's eyes when I look at them, which is why I never liked seeing Marcus in his. They're completely opaque and mirrored; mine are simply black.

When these glasses are the only thing I'm wearing, it can be reassuring to know that people can't see my eyes.

They are liberating.

I can watch, I can stare.

My attention can linger in a way that would be most inappropriate if people saw me doing it.

I glance at men, giving them a quick up and down, and then positively stare at their dicks.

I look at women in the same way, but that's another story.

I wouldn't be so brave and bold if they could see my eyes.

I love looking at cocks.

This particular afternoon we headed to The Meadow, ostensibly to sunbathe, wearing our hide-our-eyes shades.

"Shall we lie down here?" Marcus suggested when we'd barely entered the field.

"You don't think further from the gate?" We were doing that thing we do, pondering the best location. Does everyone do that, or do some people just decisively sit without any dithering?

"No. No point in walking all that way," his voice dropped to a whisperer. "We can see everyone clearly from here, and they can see *you.*"

Sure enough, everyone coming or going had to pass through the same gate. The Meadow is a few acres, and less than fifteen people were in the field, all fairly well spread out.

We were surrounded in all directions by the sounds, smells, and sights of nature, rolling meadows, ancient hedgerows, and a dense curtain of trees. When no one spoke, you only heard birds and insects. We were not far from civilization, but the topography blotted out any sound of traffic.

"Here will be fine," I agreed.

We laid out our towels and plopped ourselves on top of them. I sprayed Marc with sun protection, and then he rubbed suntan cream all over me. On our backs, with a clear view of everything around us.

Almost immediately, another man parked his towel about eight yards down from us; he lay on his stomach with his body propped up on his elbows, giving himself the perfect view of the bottom of my feet. Not just my feet, of course.

My legs were only spread a few inches apart, but he had the perfect view.

I relaxed, knowing that's what the men wanted to see.

I wasn't about to cover myself.

Shortly after the first man settled, a few others pitched themselves within our immediate vicinity. One at a time, most of the men stood up and walked about, finally relocating themselves nearer to us.

You know what I said about choosing the best location; we watched it in action as everyone in The Meadow slowly moved.

They didn't all do it at once, and each one made it look as if it was a pure coincidence: their patches of grass had suddenly become uncomfortable, and the slope of the field in our corner was just right, all of a sudden.

I am pleased they go through this masquerade. If they'd just walked towards us and sat down, surrounding us as soon as we arrived, it would have been intimidating, and we would have left.

Polite social behavior requires a certain dance to allow people to feel comfortable.

A group gathered just a few feet from the first man. They weren't subtle. They stared at me and seemed to be talking about me, but. I couldn't hear what they were saying.

One man in the group stood up; he wasn't the only thing standing up. His erection protruded proudly at a right angle to his body.

He had a fit body and an impressive huge cock, long and thick. I've seen a lot of dick in my life, and this one still managed to impress me.

The owner of it talked with his friends but repeatedly glanced over at me. He wrapped his hand around the base of his mouthwatering erection, the implication being I could have it if I wanted it.

I did want it, of course.

No one covers up in the Meadow; this is not a place for hiding, wrapped in a towel.

From the surreptitious cover of my opaque glasses, I saw many erections and men touching their dicks. I like that view.

I had the urge to touch my pussy but didn't feel confident enough to put on such a display right then (that's another story).

I wanted the men to see my pussy.

I wanted to show them I'd completely shaven in preparation.

So I spread my legs wider, just a little, and then a little more.

My audience undoubtedly would appreciate this, not just the clear view of my hairless lips but the gesture of parting my legs for their benefit.

While all this was going on Marc and I chatted casually about this and that.

Who are we to sit in judgment?

Marcus was thoroughly enjoying himself and nude. He enjoys watching and loves seeing his wife get lots of attention.

Completely naked, but for the glasses, I lay next to him.

"You should open your legs a little more," he'd whisper to me. "Spread them wider, so they get a great view."

I'd reply, "I can't; I'm too embarrassed."

"You're not. You know that they like to see," he'd coax. He never seemed to understand that much as I might enjoy putting on a brazen show, and I knew they'd all love it. I also felt shy. It was difficult to overcome the initial embarrassment.

I like watching them.

I love seeing those guys with their hard cocks, touching themselves.

"You should touch yourself too. They'd like to see that."

Yes.

I'd love to do that

I can't do that.

Can I?

I wasn't ready to put on a show, but I relaxed and enjoyed myself. I got more comfortable, which involved spreading my legs a little bit wider and a little wider still.

No mistaking my arousal. My swollen, moist lips and hard clitoris poking out on display would be obvious for all to see.

"Do you want to touch yourself?" Marcus asked.

In my mind, I'd like to.

"I can't do it."

Marcus could've touched me, and we could've put on a show together, but I wasn't going to ask.

He was lying there looking completely disinterested, which I knew was an act.

Our conversation occurred in whispers without us moving as we watched the world around us.

"Why don't *you* go over there and join them."

I couldn't believe he suggested that; it required more nerve than I possessed. The longer we stayed there, the more I wanted to be a part of what those men had to offer, but the thought of initiating things: Impossible.

"You know I can't do that," I said. "Why don't you go over and talk to them?"

Marc lay there looking every bit as if he wasn't bothered one way or the other; he played it cool. Did I want it more than he did?

I wished the men would come to me, but it didn't look like there were going to do that.

Everyone wanted me to make the first move, everyone except me.

More men arrived in the Meadow while we lay there, but still, there might have been no more than thirty people in that field. Most were quite close to me, and a few were farther away.

We all knew what we wanted. The field was large enough, so those who weren't interested in playing or watching didn't have to watch or listen.

My shaven pussy was wet and swollen and wanted some contact.

They wanted it; I wanted it.

My husband wasn't going to make it happen. He wanted me to go get involved with those men and leave him watching where he lay.

I took a deep breath, gathered up my courage, stood up, and walked toward the group of men, looking directly at the man who was still standing with his massive dick in his hand.

This small crowd of strangers looked friendly and welcoming.

Still, thank goodness for my dark glasses that prevented eye contact and helped conceal my embarrassment.

"May I join you?" I asked and continued as if the answer were a given. I sat down on the grass between two men, and the standing man sat with me.

What next?

I hadn't thought about what next, but I wasn't here for polite conversation; it could get embarrassing, so I took action.

"May I?" I asked, looking at the big dick that had been making my water and my pussy moist. Without waiting for an answer, I leaned forwards to take it in my mouth. I got onto my hands and knees, and he fell backward onto his elbows for support.

Amidst the audience of strangers within touching distance and with my husband some ten yards away, I gave this handsome, fit, well-hung stranger a blowjob.

I licked the head first, swirling the tip of my tongue around it for all to see. Then with my tongue outstretched, I moved down the shaft. Finally, I took as much of it as possible into my mouth.

I loved doing this: blowing a stranger in front of more strangers.

I loved doing it because it was outrageous, shocking, and not the sort of thing a nice girl is supposed to do.

It's the stuff fantasies are made of, straight out of a porn script.

Being the star actress in my very own porn show turned me on.

Real life isn't like a porn film. However, it's full of things that don't go as they do in your imagination. If I were the scriptwriter, I'd also have fucked that man, but that wasn't to happen.

Within not enough time, I heard him groan.

"Oh, I'm coming," he warned. His whole body tensed in the way they do. His cock jerked in my mouth, followed by the flow of his creamy seed.

As turned on as I was, I continued to suck it hard until his orgasm had subsided. I sucked and licked until he was clean and dry, and I swallowed every last drop—much to the delight of our audience.

I heard mutterings of approval, queries about whether he was *really* coming in my mouth, filling it with cream, and whether I would spit or swallow.

There was admiration for the guy who was getting this fantastic blowjob. *Good girl.*

"I'm so sorry," he said sheepishly.

No man likes to come that quickly, and it may have been worse for him with an audience watching this performance. "I'd been so turned on for such a long time," he added as an excuse.

Smiling at well-hung-handsome with his excuses, I said nothing but thought, what next? That erotic excitement was all over too quickly; who next?

The men sitting alongside me were all holding their erections, pleasuring themselves, and at the same time presenting them to me.

Without studying my options (not considering them at all), I made a move on the nearest man to me. There was another dick to fill my mouth. It allowed me to present myself as a horny, up-for-anything, good-time girl and removed the need to speak or make eye contact with these strangers.

I used one hand to keep myself stable, palm flat against the floor. With my free hand, I reached out to find something else to hold; I grasped for one of the erections nearby and took hold of it.

Without a doubt, it was exciting to be surrounded by men eager to play with me, but I wanted some pleasure myself. I also wanted to feel a firm hand or a warm mouth against my private pleasure zone. I wanted to groan and scream uncontrollably with irrepressible delight.

Before I had any time to consider how to move this open-air party up another level, I noticed that my husband had moved closer to watch over the proceedings.

He stood just outside the group. His right hand moved slowly up and down the length of his member. At such times, I may be tempted to wonder why I give any attention to other guys because my husband has a 100% guaranteed pussy-pleasuring penis.

It never fails to deliver.

It's as hard as I want and for as long as required.

Why am I here?

The answer was, for the fun of it.

Great sex isn't just about having a great lover; it is related to the environment, the situation, and the circumstances. It is about what's happening in my mind and not just in my cunt.

It's the fun of playing away and the excitement of something new or someone new.

"Melissa," he said in a gravelly voice. "Why don't you get on that man's cock and fuck him."

I'm certainly not submissive, however, at times, it can be quite nice to defer to my husband's advice. Whenever my husband says something like that, he has a good reason.

Perhaps he liked the look of a man's friendly face, but more likely because of a magnificent penis.

Marcus likes to see massive phallic objects entering me. Whether it's a cock or a dildo, he always chooses something larger than I'd choose for myself!

It never ceases to amaze me that such massive members slip in so easily.

I'm going to sit on the biggest cock in the group because that's what I want!

My husband's suggestion removes responsibility from me and makes it appear that I'm doing things because my husband wants me to do them, when, in fact, I'm doing it because I want to.

I'm only doing this because I want to.

I had no loyalty to the cocks I was currently attending.

I was happy to drop them like hot coals, I owed the men nothing.

I moved to the man my husband suggested, although a brief thought dashed through my mind as it often does at times like this: there is a chance that he doesn't want me to do that. Not every man in the group wants to play; some want to watch, and some have wives and don't wish to cheat on them.

Marcus handed me a condom.

The man showed no sign of objection, so I slipped a condom over his penis and slid myself over the top. Marcus had chosen a huge whopper; he's so predictable.

As he lay flat on the grass, I worked my way up and down the man's shaft for a few minutes, savoring the sensations of my slit, of being filled and stretched completely.

I was free to have a good look around, which is the wonderful thing about this position. Thank goodness for those glasses.

What turned me on the most in that situation was seeing and watching the other men in the field, those little further away. Men who were not part of this group and had not come over to join the fun had the hardest erections.

I love to see that; I love to see men, plural, aroused. And a man working his cock with his own hand, gently stroking, tugging, or more urgently fucking their own fist.

When I act out the porn show for their gaze, this becomes the perfect erotic situation for me. Guaranteed to get my skin hot, my pulse racing, and my pussy soaking.

I am the star of the sexual debauchery show, and my male audience loves me.

Not everyone is shy in coming forward, and a couple of other men arrive to stand at the periphery of the group, which had started as a predominantly heterogeneous group but had become a multiracial, mixed-aged, melting pot of man flesh.

For my part, I've got one in my pussy, but I can do that at home, so I waggle my finger at the newcomers to come in a little closer, making it clear I want to take them in hand (and mouth).

Wrapping my fingers around the two new members, I guide one of them to my tongue. I lick around the head and then suck him between my lips as hard and as deep as I can. It was not as easy as it sounds because I was so turned on I needed to breathe slowly and move on the hard cock inside me.

It wouldn't take long before my orgasm would be unstoppable, but I didn't want it like this.

As aroused as I was, I needed to be pounded hard and banged into the ground so I could really feel it.

I needed to change positions and possibly have a different partner though he needed to be big after this guy had stretched me so. So, I sadly had to release my grip on my two new friends in order to avoid toppling over with my need to move.

Drawing on a certain amount of self-control and willpower, I gave my current lover a peck on the cheek; I carefully withdrew from the member in my pussy.

"Who wants to fuck me from behind?" I asked as I got down on my hands and knees next to where I'd been playing.

You see, I can speak if I need to, and there is a particular urgency to my needs.

Immediately there was movement, men shifting about and rustling in their bags, looking for their own supplies of condoms, no doubt. I trusted my husband to watch over the safety of the situation, ensuring that whoever came behind me was using the proper protection; risky sex is something I don't do.

On my hands and knees on the grass, I looked at that my husband.

I couldn't see his eyes, of course, behind those mirrored sun shades, but I could see from his stance, from his hand on his dick, and the smile on his mouth that he was enjoying it as much as I was.

I liked putting on the show, and he liked watching the show.

I liked being fucked by strangers – lots of strangers; he liked watching me getting fucked by strangers, strangers with big dicks.

I didn't look to see who was behind me; it didn't matter anyway.

You can't judge a lover based on his looks, many of the very best sexual partners I've had turn out to be in surprising packages. I've learned not to judge people based on their looks or their age.

I put my own hand down to my pussy and felt his latex-covered length sliding into me. It needed no hands to guide it, as my hole was slippery and wet. I just liked feeling it being filled with a monster dick, an alien invader.

The man knew how to fuck in the doggy position.

For the first couple of thrusts, his movement was slow, the next couple slightly faster and much deeper. I felt his torso against my buttocks, and his balls bounce against me. His dick was long and thick, judging by how I was filled.

"Oh, yes!" The words flew out of my mouth with my panting breath. I wanted him to know how good this felt, wanting them all to know.

His thrusts got faster, more urgent. Was that for him? It was definitely what I wanted, and I thrust back to meet him.

"Fuck me hard, harder," I commanded. Not so much instruction as me voicing my thoughts, making it clear I was on the edge, and more of the same would take me over it.

Unrelenting, long hard thrusts pounded me.

Withdrawing until his cock was out, pushing it back in all the way home.

A varying speed, a few fast, a few languid.

A few shallow, a few deep.

Holding me at the edge, and the longer I stayed there, the more intense the building orgasm was going to be.

"Fuck me hard; now I'm going to come!" Not a command, a plea.

I wanted what I wanted, and he was already giving it to me.

His hands gripped tighter around my hips, and he gave it to me hard and fast. Harder and faster. My cunt was clenching, the juices flowing, and there was no holding back.

"Yes! Yes!" I was very vocal and loud, and most of the noises were not words but primitive cries of pleasure.

Some of the men surrounding us also came at the same time, on their hands, in their towels, or letting the spunk spill over the grass.

I didn't steal a glance at the man behind me, but I felt those familiar movements, the shudder that ripped through his whole body, the way his thrusts suddenly stammered and halted.

I knew he'd come too.

Without looking at my cuckold husband, I was certain he had *not* come.

He'd savor this sight and hope we might do more later. Ultimately he delayed his fulfillment until the very end, knowing that I am always insatiable and always there for him.

BOOK THREE

The Nudist Soc at The Beach

P*art 1*
The Big Idea Sounds Like A Plan

Dave looked at the washing machine mournfully. "I'm going to have to give in and find out how this thing works." His arms were full of dirty washing, a veritable grubby cotton mountain, which he dumped on the floor in front of the machine. "I'm just about out of clean underwear."

"I'm sure you can figure it out," said Mark, standing next to him in the kitchen area of the open-plan living space. "I'd help you, but I'm cooking."

Mark was in charge of catering according to their rota. A pile of ramen noodles awaited rehydration, and the full kettle was making its way to boiling point.

Fine dining and gaming, student style.

"I'm selecting games, so don't ask me about pants," Fred called over. He was sitting on the floor surrounded by wires, boxes, and retro video games next to the TV at the other end of the living room. Anyway, programming is your thing, isn't it, Dave?"

"Computer programming, yes. This is a machine, so it's your field, Mr. Robot Man," Dave responded, addressing the comment to Fred, who was majoring in artificial intelligence.

As if out of a TV advert set in a launderette, Dave rolled up his T-shirt and pulled it over his head, revealing his slim, lean figure. He then undid his trousers and pulled them off. No undergarments.

He'd gone commando due to his dirty laundry crisis, which was typical midway through the second week of the second year of his full-time University degree.

After removing his socks, while bent over, he picked up the laundry off the floor and pushed the whole lot into the washing machine.

Completely naked, he addressed his fellow roommates who shared the student accommodation with him. "Thought I'd wear my birthday suit to Thursday night games night tonight."

"A washing machine is a domestic appliance, not AI, not by any stretch of the imagination." Fred stood up and walked towards the two men in the kitchen. "An interesting choice of clothing, Dave."

At that moment, Michael arrived and walked into the room.

His eyes widened; whether it was due to the naked man in the kitchen or the mountain of ready meals was about to become evident. "Goodness, Mark, dinner looks good, but I hope that's not the dress code."

"What I was thinking! No. Dave's out of clothes; that's all," Mark replied. "The same guy who can bring down satellites with his hacking skills, who can code in multiple languages, can't operate a washing machine."

"I put off learning how to use the machine until the last minute, that's all." With concentration etched on his face, Dave continued to poke at the buttons on the machine. "How hard can it be?"

"Right now, I gotta wonder if you're talking about your dick, mate. And I don't wanna know."

It was early in the semester, and this was only the second Thursday night the boys had stayed at home in their new accommodation. The small terraced house was home to four students from the School of Computer Science.

"How many second-year computer science undergraduates does it take to load a washing machine? I'm sure there's a joke in there."

"Not sure, but I'm gonna guess the answer might be four," Dave said.

"One to get his kit off."

"One to read the instructions."

"One to push the buttons."

"And the last one for project management."

THE MACHINE WAS WHIRRING, the boys were sitting at the table with their instant noodles and an assortment of cutlery, and the conversation turned to the elephant in the room.

Not so much an elephant as a snake of the trouser snake variety.

"That's a hell of a ding dong you got hanging there."

"I'm not gay, but if any of you boys would like to suck on my salami, please don't hesitate to ask."

"Why should any of us want to do that?"

"I don't know, but it doesn't see any other action. And let's face it is not likely to. I'm an undergraduate science student, six foot tall and lanky enough to hide behind a lamp stand."

Lanky, he was not. He'd matured, passed the lanky stage, and was filling out nicely with chiseled features, a flat stomach, and defined muscles: everything a girl wants and more.

Most importantly of all, he had a major asset, his ultra-long schlong. If it got more of an airing in the world, it would certainly draw attention.

"I feel a bit sorry for it hanging there like a third leg, all unnecessary and unloved." Fed sighed. "Sorry, but not *that* sorry."

"I'm not gay either, seeing as we're doing the *'I'm not gay but...'* thing," said Michael. "I might just take you up on that if, and only if, I have to resort to a plan B."

"You mean you have a plan A?" The boys stared at him quizzically.

"I have an amazing plan A. The plan that will get us surrounded by naked chicks. And I am so confident about plan A that '*I'm not gay but…*' I promise I personally will suck your cock until it pops if my plan doesn't work."

"So I'm on to a win-win?" Dave said with an uncertain smile.

"You are, indeed, Dave, my boy." Michael exuded an unnatural level of confidence.

"Prey tell," Fred asked.

"Plan A goes like this. There are funds available for student societies. Uni-socs aren't socks that can be worn by any student regardless of gender."

"Not unit shocks, either." Mark offered unhelpfully.

"They are university societies. We should have one dedicated to getting us laid by babes," Michael continued to draw out every last moment, keeping his pals in suspense as he worked his way around to the nuts and bolts of the scheme.

"I'm with you. A uni-soc called *Girls for Geeks,* but how will it work? We don't have the money to pay them."

Undeterred, Michael continued, "I'm a registered and fully insured driver for the university's student union bus. I can use that bus to go anywhere at any time, within reason, for student union business."

"Okay. I'm not getting how you being a bus driver gets any of us laid?" Dave said what they were all thinking.

Fred hung on Michael's every word, open-mouthed.

"It works like this. We need to set up a nudist group. The student's nudist society, SNS, or something catchy like that."

"And the society needs more members," Fred tittered.

"Not exactly more members; we've got four here." Dave stood up and waved his member around. "Everyone loves a double entendre thrust in their face."

"Seriously, fellas, we want women, but we'll have to take everyone who wants to sign up, boy, girls, and other genders. And our first trip must be pretty soon before the weather turns to freezing. So our first trip will be to the nudist beach, and I'm thinking next week.

"So we've got a few days to get the student nudist society off the ground. We need members; we need a website. After all, we are computer geeks; we have to have a website."

"I like the idea. Once naked babes surround us, we are one big step closer to the goal." Mark was well into this plan.

"Maybe you guys have higher aspirations than me," said Fred. "I'd be happy with the goal of being surrounded by naked girls. Nothing else has to happen."

"You can imprint the image on your eyes and play it back later if you want. For your single-handed pleasure." Michael teased him.

"So, your plan is the four of us fill a minibus with babes and dudes who are gonna come to the beach with us, and we've all got to take off our clothes." Fred wanted to be quite sure he understood.

"Exactly. It sounds like a good plan, right? I can't promise anyone will sit on your sausage but surrounded by hot naked babes or even nude computer science girls, it's bound to happen, isn't it? Girls must get horny too! Right?" Dave was sold on the idea; after all, public nudity wasn't a problem for him.

"We might get just dudes," Fred mumbled.

"Don't want to put a downer on things, but the idea is fundamentally flawed." Mark addressed Fred as he spoke. "Here we are, three guys, sitting in jeans and T-shirts with one wacko-nude guy, surrounded by instant noodles, cheap beer, and video games. How are things gonna change? We'll still be the geeks who are one hundred percent skilled in a total inability to talk to the opposite sex. The only difference I see is that it will be a similar scene but at the seaside. Will anybody join us?"

"Well, we will have a website," Dave said hopefully. "And incredible optimism."

"We must sell a dream, and it isn't to sit naked in the cold." Michael had apparently given this some detailed thought. "It's about being radical and idealistic. It's smashing capitalism and combating consumerism. Reject society's norms to save the planet. Have you seen how hot some of those political girls are? The sociology undergrads and political science students. The eco-warriors, with their colored hair and dreadlocks. They'll be up for it."

"You might just be onto something," Dad narrowed his eyes and banged his fist on the table. "You sly dog!"

"Michael, have you got your eye on some punk girl?" Mark asked.

"Not one in particular, but as a whole breed, they're quite sexy." Michael winked. "And let's face it, the conservative girls are not gonna be doing this. So, we have got to appeal to those who are already interested in making waves, doing things differently, and standing out from the crowd. We're selling the dream. The revolution. Not a cold beach in October!"

"And the following gathering will have to be indoors," Fred added with a shiver.

Part 2

Promoting the Nudist Student Society

After a late-night gaming session turned into an early morning horror film fest with more potato snacks than anyone could eat, the tired young men turned their minds to the new student club they wanted to set up.

By mid-morning, posters were on display, and a website was live.

They started work on developing a website alongside their gaming. This team of computer science students could have done a basic site within an hour. There was considerable delay, however, when it came to images and research. The research involved studying the websites of other nudist groups, notably their picture galleries. Searching the term "student nudist" provided a bounty of research materials beyond their wildest dreams and enough to keep them going for the weekend.

Several hours were lost browsing and commenting on other nudist websites.

While they knew they couldn't use copyrighted images from other sites, there was no harm in looking at those other sites for ideas.

Lot. Of. Ideas.

Looking slowly and carefully at pictures of naked college girls was an enjoyable pastime though nothing as explicit could go on the college website. Many full-frontal naked women of their age would make for an excellent website but wouldn't be acceptable on the university server.

Instead, their images had to be subtle and humorous, such as deformed vegetables hiding the real meat, that sort of thing.

And, more importantly, images of babes wouldn't attract the girls they hoped would participate in the group.

SUNDAY PROVIDED THE catalysis they needed.

There was a top news article perfect for launching the nudist group into the spotlight and grabbing the attention of the politically-minded, rad girls at college.

Do something about this outrage. Show your solidarity. Protest against exploited child labor. Don't wear clothes made by children working for a dollar a day.

Go bare!

Get Your Kit Off.

The launch of the university nudist society was a great success.

Its amusing website lacked any nudity at all. At the same time, its poster campaign around college called on students to go nude to show international solidarity with young people in other parts of the world.

It attracted attention.

They quickly sold out of seats on the minibus for the beach trip. There was a limited number of places that filled quickly.

The boys administered the booking list with a close eye; they wanted to ensure a good proportion of female students getting seats. After all, they already had four men going.

The success of the group was measured in terms of female interest. And they were overwhelmed by the female supporters of the *Get Your Kit Off* campaign.

PART 3

The Bus

The day had arrived, and success meant the bus was packed with an even number of men and women. Surely it could not get any better?

At least three apprehensive passengers sat on the university minibus on the way to the beach. That morning they acknowledged the one thing they hadn't discussed; a flaw in the bright idea and a big one. The only thing that could improve the event was if they didn't have to get their clothes off.

The guys were all apprehensive about being exposed.

It seemed like a plan full of holes.

Cold weather would ensure they offered unattractive pale goose flesh and shriveled-up genitals. And that might be even worse than over-excitement and embarrassing erections.

How were they going to look good in front of the girls?

More likely, they were going to make themselves a laughingstock.

They were en route, on the bus, to total humiliation.

This was the concern of the three men. The fourth housemate, the one who gave birth to this great idea, was driving.

"Thank goodness, I see the sun," said Lucy.

"It's warm on this bus," said Sara. "We should strip off for the journey in case it's too cold when we get there." She pulled her jumper off over her head.

Though the boys held their breaths for a moment, she had a bikini top underneath. Her exposed skin and wobbling cleavage looked good, but a bikini top wasn't what they had in mind. Hopefully, it would come off too.

Another girl followed her example, pulling off layer after layer as if she was an overly packed Christmas present. A fluffy pink jumper, a purple cotton top that matched her purple hair color, a pink vest.

When the vest came off there was just skin. Tanned skin, no strap marks. Small pert breasts with dark nipples like giant raisins.

"Breathe," Fred whispered ever so quietly.

Purple hair was sitting next to black hair. Two punky-looking girls came along together. The boys forgot their concerns as the dark-haired girl pulled her dress over her head.

The boys didn't need to worry about running the show. They were no longer in charge of the group. Once they launched their baby, new members took the student soc and ran with it.

As soon as the bus was parked alongside the secluded stretch of beach, they were out of the van and stripping off as if it were an everyday activity.

The girls were uninhibited.

The boys could have stayed in their clothes, and no one was paying them any attention, but they would have looked like peeping Toms.

Michael wasn't having any slacking off from his team. It was his idea, and he'd driven them to it, literally.

Part 4

Paddling

The beach was a pleasant sand and stone mix in a bay sheltered from the exposed sea breezes. Inland, the only road was little more than a track through dense trees.

They were miles from the nearest town, at the ideal place for a nudist beach.

The remote location required a car to get there, and there was a car park right next to the beach.

"Remember what Mick said. The secret is not to think of them as naked girls," Dave whispered to Fred and Mark as the three of them were left beside the van.

The others quickly took off to the beach, removing their clothes as they went. They'd already built a mountain of clothes and bags on the sand about fifty yards from the vehicle.

"Perhaps when they're dressed in big boots, jeans, and bagged hoodies, I could do that," said Mark looking towards the girls. "But without clothes, it's not easy."

"What would Mick know anyway?" Fred mumbled, looking terrified. He was considerably less comfortable with his body; he loitered by the van pulling out and examining spare equipment, anything to delay the inevitable stripping off.

"I'm not saying I can do it, but I will try to fit in with them." Dave was fairly comfortable with his body. After all, he's the sort of guy who does his laundry in the nude while having a video games evening with friends. But admittedly, girls weren't present.

"And just look at Mick now," he said.

They were all looking in that direction because that was where the nude girls were.

Michael seemed right at home in the middle of them, setting up a game of beach volleyball. He strode out with the girls, displaying his confidence as if he'd been to nudist beaches many times before. After hurriedly stripping his clothes off, showing how comfortable he was with his body, he relaxed completely.

"Try not to think of them as naked girls, just as mates," Dave hissed before heading over to join the fun.

Mark followed hastily. Without any sign of self-consciousness, he launched himself into beach volleyball with the girls and a couple of new blokes from the Faculty of Social Science.

DAVE THOUGHT HE SAW one of the girls admiringly looking at him, but he might have imagined it.

With his clothes thrown onto the pile, for a moment, he wondered if they were all labeled but remembered he was a grown man, and name labels were left behind with a school uniform a few years ago.

He wasn't a team player but emboldened by his nudity, he glanced at the girl he thought was looking.

She didn't look away. She damn well approached wearing a big smile and nothing else.

"Do you fancy paddling? she asked.

Bloody hell, would I, he thought, but just replied," Yes, let's go."

She wasn't the sort of girl Dave imagined would look twice at him.

She was tall and slim with a figure that would look right on an action girl in one of his video games. You know, wide hips and a pinched waist as if pulled in by a corset? Shelley had one of those even when naked. Big round boobies that wobbled in a distracting but extremely mouth-wateringly pleasant manner topped off her appearance.

With his own attribute jiggling and slapping against his legs as they walked at a swift pace toward the sea, Dave realized he also had something to display proudly.

The water felt quite chilly on their toes.

"I'm Shelley, and you're Dave, aren't you?"

"Yes," said Dave, as predicted, his mind went blank. His brain wasn't wired for chatting with naked girls.

Shelley was blond, her hair hung freely like everything else, and she chose him.

Shelley grabbed his palm, screeched, and giggled at the first feeling of the chilly sea tickling the bottoms of their feet and lapping over their toes.

"Come on, let's be brave together," she said.

The water wasn't icy; it just took a little bit of getting used to as they were just out of their warm van, socks, and trainers.

Together they splashed into the water, only to just above their ankles. While they acclimatized to the temperature, they held onto each other. Her feminine curves and more-than-a-hand-full breasts touched him.

The result was predictable.

Despite cold seawater chilling his lower limbs, the blood rushed to the central erogenous zone of his body.

"Oh no!" He helplessly tried mind over matter to conjure up thoughts of a non-sexual nature. But he was defeated.

He felt a little embarrassed but also excited. A part of him wanted Shelley to see what he'd got and know the effect she was having on him. If the worst came to the worst, he could always plunge himself into the cold water.

"Do you think this helps? Us taking our clothes off and doing a bit of paddling?" She asked,

"Helps?" He looked blank, thinking only with his hard dick.

"Helps the world situation. The exploitation of kids. Labor conditions in foreign countries."

"Yes, of course. Here we are facing each other. Breaking down barriers." Dave knew his cock was pointing to the clouds. Even though she was looking at his face, she must have seen it too.

He was determined to stand boldly there as if it was the most natural thing. And the conversation was a bit easier as they moved on to a topic he'd rehearsed.

"It helps with breaking down barriers," he continued. "We've never spoken to each other before; we probably never would have done it if it wasn't for this. And we're proving that we can get along without clothes made in one of those places. So on a microscopic personal level, it's helping."

She smiled, and he thought she looked a little flushed.

"I think there's a different benefit," she said. "I would never have met you if it wasn't this, and I think you look rather cute." She looked down at his broom handle as she carried on talking. "You look quite sexy, standing here completely naked."

She was flirting with him, big time.

That was it; there was no controlling the blood flow to Dave's horny barometer.

It started to pulse and bob as it became the center of attention.

He liked it a lot.

He liked the way her breasts were much bigger than they should be on her body, and her pale skin looked a little bit red when it shouldn't. She was obviously a bit flushed, too; embarrassed or excited?

Dave was about to run into the sea, at least waist deep, to hide his bulging embarrassment when Shelley stopped him.

She moved closer to him, took his hands in hers, and pushed her body against him.

If he were going to do what she expected him to do, he would have to stoop his head, as she was considerably shorter.

So he did. He bent down and kissed her.

Her soft breasts were against his chest, and his hard cock pushed into her stomach.

They kissed; they snogged.

Her warm wet tongue invaded his mouth; her tits squashed against him.

This was going somewhere, and Dave was pretty sure of that.

Part 5

At The Van

Fred continued to loiter at the van, even after his housemates left him. He examined every bit of equipment packed inside.

He was stalling for time and digging deep inside to find reserves of self-confidence.

But he was still enjoying himself because just a short distance away, buck-naked girls were running around and jumping up in the air; it was an excellent show.

Nude beach volleyball was a good spectator sport.

Not everyone had joined in.

Fred saw the silhouette of Shelley with her hourglass figure and Dave with his embarrassing hard-on as if holding a french stick.

With the sun behind them on the horizon, he couldn't see them clearly. They were standing on the edge of the seashore. He watched as their silhouettes merged to form one.

"Dave, you lucky dog," Fred muttered and rearranged the growing erection within his pants. "Mick might be the brains of the operation, but you had the secret weapon."

Dave was first to the action, but Fred was sure Mark and Michael would follow, being surrounded by the rest of the group, playing bouncing ball games and having nude fun. They appeared at ease with the rest of the girls as they threw themselves into the activities. It seemed to be a boy versus girls match, four-a-side.

Four? So one girl was missing.

Just as Fred registered this in his mind, one of the girls came up to him. She was only partially undressed; she'd taken off her jeans. A long baggy T-shirt, as big as a dress, covered who knows what.

What could he say? But he didn't have to come up with anything.

"Are you going to join us on the beach?" she asked, "or are you hanging out by the van for the day?"

"Yeah, I'm coming over. I just like to be organized. It's a bit of OCD, you know."

"Have you done this sort of thing before?"

Fred felt put on the spot, already vulnerable. Honesty was the best policy to deal with this unfamiliar situation. "No, I've never done this kind of thing before, and frankly, I'm a little bit nervous about it."

"Me too. I liked the idea, but I feel a bit embarrassed now that I'm here." She paused and bit her lower lip. You could stay in the van with me for a little while. We could get to know each other, and we might feel a bit more comfortable then.

Fred thought about this suggestion, but his lack of response must have been misread as the girl spoke again after a short silence.

"Please. I don't know anybody here, and it would make me feel better if I knew you."

"Yeah. Good idea." He should have responded faster. *What is wrong with me?*

"You seem to know everyone," she said as they slipped side-by-side into the minibus.

"Four of us share a house," he offered by explanation. "Apart from that, the others are just faces at school."

They entered the van, sliding next to each other on the rear seats.

She said, "I'll take my clothes off if you take off yours. Then we'll be naked with one other person, and it doesn't seem like such a big deal. Okay?"

It may not seem like much of a big deal to her but to him being naked and alone with a warm-blooded woman was even more daunting than being exposed to a crowd of people.

No, scratch that; the thought of being naked with a crowd of people was terrifying and getting worse the longer he had delayed it.

"Yes," he said, being a man of few words right then. They both lifted up their T-shirts simultaneously, and after Fred had discarded his, he realized this left the girl sitting in only a tiny thong.

When did Fred slip into this parallel universe where he could sit next to a girl in so little and not even know her name?

And without any suggestion that money would exchange hands!

Fred, of course, was still wearing his jeans.

She stood up in the cramped space, with her back to him, and slipped off her G-string. "Are you curious as to why I came here on my own?" she asked with her back still towards him.

This hadn't crossed his mind; he had concerns of his own; he was feeling hot, bothered, and aroused and was about to get naked with a girl.

Perhaps it was strange behavior for a girl. Girls always seem to gather and move together in a sort of mob.

"Shall I tell you?" she prompted, turning to look at him as she sat back down beside him.

"Yes, sure."

"Well, you need to take your jeans off first." She looked him up and down. "After all, I'm naked and about to expose my inner self as well as my body. The least you can do is take your clothes off too."

It was a confined space, which made removing his shoes, socks, jeans, and underwear difficult, but it had to be done. At least it felt like a private space, inside the van, as opposed to a very public and exposed beach outside.

As he got his kit off, she continued to speak.

"I've always had these fantasies about nudism. It's not the politics that appealed to me. Just, purely, well," she stammered and blushed furiously. "It sounds dead sexy to be naked with strangers like this."

Did she say what he thought she said? Was she flirting?

She continued, "Don't you find it a bit sexy? A turn-on?"

Part 6

A Turn On

Was she kidding?

Fred was naked in a van with a naked girl. How could it not be turned on?

And if he denied it? His rock-hard cock promised to contradict him.

He couldn't believe it as the girl's hands moved her hand across him, skimming over his body and aiming straight toward his crotch.

His cock was so hard it strained to be touched by this woman, by anyone!

Her intentions were clear, and she was wrapping her fingers around his cock; with her other hand, she explored his body.

"That's better. I'm starting to feel more relaxed already." She smiled, and he looked into her eyes, which twinkled with naughtiness. "I'm getting to know you better, and I feel more relaxed already. What about you?"

"Perhaps we should have started with names." People often started with kissing too, but he wasn't going to complain about a woman holding his cock.

"Perhaps," she agreed. "I'm Christina."

"Fred." Few words. He reached out to caress her firm young breasts gently.

She pushed her body into his hands, squashing her tits against his palms.

Fred couldn't believe his luck, a willing naked woman beside him.

He stroked her soft skin.

She moved in closer to him, cuddling up. Like a dream, this girl took control. She didn't expect anything from him but forced herself upon him. Finally, kissing him, touching him all over.

Fred was glad to be used in this way. He sat there willingly, wishing and willing Christina to do whatever she wanted with him.

Before he knew it, she was bending over. What was she doing? Where was she going? She couldn't have dropped something on the floor. Her head was sliding down his body. Was she really going to?

O. M. G.

Her mouth neared his cock, and her tongue teased the head. She licked and tickled before sealing her lips around it. She then worked her way down, engulfing it in her moist warm cavity.

Fred felt like he was going to explode already.

His hands were upon the woman, but he was barely in control of his mind and never dreamed such a thing would happen to him.

He hadn't even gotten onto the damned beach. He'd only just gotten his clothes off, and none of his friends had seen him nude, which was a relief.

There were windows in the minibus, but no one was around, so it was almost as good as being in private with a naked woman.

And she was giving him a blowjob. Days don't get any better.

Her head went up and down above his cock.

He was sure she would want more than just a mouthful of his cum. And he was equally sure she'd be getting a mouthful soon if she continued much longer.

He threaded his fingers through her hair. In part, he wanted to push her head down onto his cock and partly to pull it away before it all became too much.

He pulled her off, and she looked up at him — her mouth open, eyes wide with desire, looking wanton and every bit as turned on as he felt.

She looked like a woman from his fantasies rather than from his college: unlike those unapproachable girls.

"Do you like that?" She grinned.

She damn well knew he did, and she stuck her tongue out suggestively. It was a long tongue that could almost reach the tip of his dick.

Oh, fuck me!

"You damn well know I do."

"Do you have any condoms?"

"Yes, in my jeans; in the pocket." He couldn't believe it.

Michael insisted they shared a packet this morning, three each, in their back pockets. Fred certainly hadn't expected to use one, and he thought of them more as novelty items to be carried around hopefully rather than something to actually use.

"Do you want to get it out then?" she suggested.

He bent down, picked his jeans up off the floor, and rummaged around. He was all fingers and thumbs. It had never been so hard to find his back pocket. Everywhere he slipped his fingers, that denim fabric seemed to be in the wrong place, just folds of blue cloth, but eventually, the shiny packet emerged between his fingers.

He was about to rip it open when she snatched it from his hand. "Allow me."

She tore the packet and tossed it to one side as she pulled out the latex rubber. She slipped it down his cock like a woman of experience and then turned her back toward him. Hovering over his hard dick, she positioned herself on top, moved his sheathed dick into place between her wet folds, and slipped straight down.

Her back towards him.

It made sense, given they were in a cramped vehicle, it seemed the best position; she may have had prior experience with minibus sex.

Fred put his arms around her, fondled her soft breasts, and honed in on her pussy with one hand. Fleetingly touching the trimmed mound, he quickly found her hard clitoris and soft, moist slit.

He stroked his fingers along the creases and either side of her labia, dipping and sliding in the slippery moistness, crossing her pleasure zone and teasing her clit.

He took pleasure from the joyful sounds, the moans of pleasure that she let out as she experienced his skilled fingers over her private party parts and his hard cock inside her.

Ecstasy.

Just as well. He wouldn't last much longer, and he didn't want to come without satisfying this lady.

That wasn't going to happen, she came.

Her thrusting becomes more urgent, her moans and screams becoming louder. Most telling of all, her pussy clamped tightly around his dick, squeezing it and feeling hotter and hotter and wetter and wetter.

Unable to control himself any longer, unable to hold back, he also came.

Part 7

By The Sea

Dave quickly felt at home, exploring the skin of his friendly companion. They molded together nicely, and Shelley seemed to delight in the way his hands held her, caressing her back, her buttocks, between her legs.

She was willing; he was willing.

They were still standing at the edge of the water. Shallow waves broke on the shore, lapped over their toes, over their feet, washing at the beach on which they stood. Then it disappeared back out to sea while the sand beneath their feet sank below them.

Returning waves washed them clean, repeating the cycle. Withdrawing as the tide was going out.

Almost oblivious to the cycle, Paul had his cock nuzzled into Shelley's soft flesh. Her hands were on him, exploring him, touching him everywhere, up the sides of his body, under his arms, under his armpits.

His armpits!

Along those arms and over his biceps, shoulders, and neck.

He felt horny.

She was horny. This was going somewhere!

She slipped her hand in between them and wrapped her fingers around his cock, gently rubbing and tugging in a most erotic way. Of course, he wanted to bury it inside, but his condoms were way back with his clothes. They were on the seashore's edge, and he didn't want to break this moment.

He reached down between her legs and found her private area. Soft, moist, warm, and so welcoming.

She parted her legs slightly to allow better access.

His fingers slipped in and out, and purrs of pleasure escaped her breath.

He needed to get in there.

The tide went out fast on this steeply sloping beach, and the water disappeared from their toes. They took a few steps further onto the drier sand, still locked in an embrace. Still locked together, they worked their way down onto the sand until they were lying together, free to explore each other's bodies.

With one hand on his dick. The free hand explored the surface of his body.

His hands were similarly touching her, feeling her curves. He was lost in the exploration of this lady, overwhelmed with pleasure, desire, and a lack of inhibition. What he'd hoped for. Every bit what he'd hoped for.

With his fingers inside her, she bucked hard, moaning, leaning towards him, thrusting her hips, grinding her pussy against his hand, and moaning.

Moaning so loud.

"I'm going to come! Oh, oh, Dave! I'm going to come! Going to come!"

Those words were like an aphrodisiac, almost guaranteed to spring him forward to that same place, whether he was there already or not.

He wanted to be with her, but he had no condoms, and he didn't wish to interrupt this moment.

He needed to come too. In fact, he was going to.

She was holding onto his cock and pulling with some urgency as her own orgasm drew closer.

He glanced around, suddenly feeling self-conscious.

Self-conscious now? It's a bit late!

The only people within sight, the only people on the beach, were the group he'd arrived with. And they were all engaged in somewhat similar activities.

Whatever happened to the volley ball game? They were all playing new ball games.

Knowing there was no audience despite the public location, hePaul decided to get inventive. "Let me lick your pussy while you come."

And like a dream, she replied, "Make it a sixty-nine."

They maneuvered into a yin-yang position: his cock in her mouth, her pussy against his face.

His lips on her clitoris, his finger inside her cunt.

His cock sucked hard.

They both thrust, and they both came, loudly and messily.

She licked and lapped his cock eagerly, sucking and swallowing every last drop as he did with her.

He licked up the moisture reveling in the taste of her, in the scent of her. She tasted way better than Mike's instant noodles.

Part 8

By The Sea

After swimming and playing in the water for some, Dave and Shelley walked up the beach, cool, refreshed, and holding hands. It was as if they'd known each other for some time, weeks, or months, not just a couple of hours.

Most of the minibus crowd were lying around looking happy and sated, tucking into picnic food and drinks.

It was evident they'd all had a good time.

But the numbers were not quite right. Who was missing?

Fred emerged from the direction of the minivan at about that same time.

Still clothed?

WTF Fred!

He was wearing his jeans and his T-shirt, although he was barefooted. Interestingly he was also holding hands with one of the girls.

How did that happen?

She was the only other person who was not naked, hiding her body under a big baggy T-shirt. Perhaps nudism and exhibitionism were not for everybody and not for all these housemates.

BOOK FOUR
My Husband's Friend

*T*his is the story of my first time as a Hotwife, and it was with my husband's lifelong friend, a man he'd grown up with.

I met and married my husband, Harry, in America. No, my name isn't Sally, before you ask. Also, he's from Europe but not a prince, and I'm not an actress. But his childhood upbringing differed greatly from mine.

With great relief, I found his family and friends were pleasant, down-to-earth people when they came over for the wedding. All perfectly normal, despite what I'd heard.

It wasn't surprising to find his brothers were all stunningly attractive, especially his identical twin brother, Carl. My hubby is gorgeous, so it must have been genetic.

And then there were his friends. Harry's friends were like brothers to him. They grew up in a tight-knit community. However, I was apprehensive about visiting them in France, not least because they'd been raised as nudists, which sounded strange to me with my American hangups.

CRAIG HADN'T BEEN ABLE to get to the wedding, so I hadn't met him before he picked us up at the airport. The thought of staying in his château and getting to know him better delighted me because it was a château, obviously. Plus, I'd heard so much about my husband's lifelong best friends; the boys had been very close.

We'd taken a lazy day to recover from the flight and the jetlag. We ate at a restaurant, drank wine, and sat up talking until far too late before collapsing for a glorious sleep in a comfy bed.

It was almost midday by the time we got out of bed after our first night in France. Harry and I showered before wandering down to the kitchen in our casuals, where we helped ourselves to petit déjeuner (orange juice, coffee, and croissants).

"I never knew northern Europe was going to be this hot," I whipped the back of my hand across my brow. I don't know why but I pictured clouds, rain, and lush green forests.

"There's a slight breeze coming through the open window." Harry chuckled. "But you're wearing too many clothes for August."

He had a point. He was wearing thin cotton joggers and a thin cotton top. While my loungewear looked similar, it was of considerably thicker cloth.

I took off my hoodie; I wore a little vest underneath and no bra: don't judge me for my fashion decisions on a relaxing European vacation.

Craig emerged from whatever he'd been up to for the morning. He must have caught the end of our discussion because he said, "Feel free to wear as little as you like or nothing at all. There's nobody here but the three of us, so just get comfortable."

My husband smiled at me. "It will be another scorcher, according to the weather forecast. And that will be hot." And then he winked.

I felt like he was daring me.

We'd wander around naked at home — in the privacy of our apartment, that was different.

"Right. That's it, then. If you two are okay with it. I'm stripping off everything. Feel free to join me." And I practically tore off my clothes;

I shed them so quickly. I acted on impulse, partly because I guessed it would be acceptable in this home of all places.

It wasn't just the room temperature or my desire to get naked between these two hunks; inexplicably, I knew our relationship required it.

It was a relief to strip because I'd become hotter and hotter since getting up that morning. I should have felt a little cooler with the breeze dancing across my skin, but I had two hunky men staring at me, which helped none.

Something else came to mind with my clothes and inhibitions lying on the floor at my feet: the close relationship the guys once had before my marriage. I didn't want my marriage to drive a wedge between them, which worried me as we prepared for the trip.

"Harry, being a twin, has taught me a thing or two; it's opened my eyes to the close bonds people can form in childhood."

"So you have been listening to me," Harry said jokingly.

"Of course," I continued. "Bonds last a lifetime. Now you two guys are as close as brothers, and that's special. You must stay close and not let our marriage spoil things."

"And as for clothes, they just get in the way. They're coming between us." My husband said as he proceeded to strip them off his and leave them in a pile covering mine, which felt perfectly natural; after all, we were married.

He had an erection. Not just a semi, not just a slightly stout one. This was a stiff rod standing rigidly upright.

No big deal, we were married. But that might have been a little odd in his friend's kitchen, and even more so as his friend was right there.

Craig shrugged, took a few steps closer, and without saying a word, he followed our example. He took off his clothes and placed them over the back of a chair at the kitchen table.

I was partly amazed and partly relieved. At least we were all equal, and no one had made an issue out of anything. No one acted as if it were strange.

It was as if being nude came perfectly naturally to the two men, so I wanted to not make it an issue.

When Craig stood naked in front of me, I sucked in a deep breath while eyeing his physique. I couldn't help blatantly looking him up and down, even if it was rude to stare, and I didn't want to make a big issue out of our nudity.

It would be difficult for any man to measure up when standing next to my buffed-up husband, but Craig was taller and broader, and his washboard abs were equally as impressive.

I didn't want to mention the elephant in the room.

Do not stare at his dick. Do. Not. Stare.

I did, of course, stare.

Well, why not? It was pointing right at me.

And it was frighteningly girthy, and I'm sure some girls would run from such a prospect.

I didn't have time to think about it because Harry lifted me off my feet and held me in his arms. I wrapped my legs around his torso, trapping his cockhead against my clit. And my swollen, moist labia snuggled against his shaft.

If I moved and wriggled, he'd have slid right in.

We were half an inch from full penetration. I wanted it, but I wasn't sure if he wanted the same — not in a kitchen and in front of his buddy.

I glanced at Craig; he was standing there watching us like this was all perfectly normal. For all I knew, it may have been normal in his life, but I'd never done anything like this. Being casually naked in front of my husband's friend was completely new to me.

And I sort of liked it.

But things didn't seem casual.

My pussy pulsed with arousal, my nipples were getting harder, and I had the urge to touch myself or touch them.

We were all turned on. As sure as I had two eyes, I'd seen two men with stiff cocks in that kitchen.

Craig wrapped his hand around the base of his erection and just held it, almost as if he were showing it to me. It refocused my attention on his dick as if I could hope to drag my gaze away.

"Put that down, as I've got other things for you to touch." My husband can sound wonderfully commanding sometimes, though he's a gentle giant.

Craig quickly complied. His hands dropped to his sides, and he stepped nearer to us.

"Join us," Harry instructed. "What's mine is mine, but I'm happy to share. And you should get to know my wife better."

His words sent a shiver of excited anticipation coursing through me.

Craig wrapped a brotherly arm around my husband's shoulder and placed a hand on my buttock so that all three of us were connected by physical contact, however slight.

The connection wasn't just a physical touch of hands against my skin. I suspected somehow incomprehensible natural forces were at work binding our relationships.

"I don't know exactly how anything's supposed to work between us after this," I said. "I'm in your hands."

It wasn't clear which of the men I was speaking to, perhaps both of them.

My urge was to kiss Harry right then; it seemed natural, but I was practically impaled on his cock and glued to his front, and I didn't think we should leave his friend, our host, out on the sidelines watching us making out while nude in his kitchen.

However, Craig had to chase us across the room as Harry snatched me away, carried me across the kitchen, and pinned me up against the fridge door. He snogged me passionately and rubbed against me like he was only just about holding it together.

I loved the out-of-control, rutting, animalistic version of my husband. His passion turned me on even more. He must have known how he affected me because hot juices gushed from my throbbing cunt, covering his dick and dampening the top of my inner thighs.

One-to-one sex didn't seem like where this was going.

I knew, as boys, the friends had always shared everything. But did they share women or porn? Did they talk through sexy fantasies and masturbate together?

Would they share me?

I sensed my nipples getting harder, my skin tingling, and my swollen, throbbing pussy getting hotter and wetter if that were possible.

All proving that reality is so much hornier than my fucking dreams. And I had a great imagination, but I hadn't imagined this. I was completely unprepared.

And then things got even better.

While the two men continued to stand, they passed me between them as if I weighed nothing. And there was a busy eruption of activity. They both covered my face and neck, and shoulders with kisses.

They took turns pinning me against the hard cold wall or sandwiching me between their two hot, sweaty bodies while they explored my body with wandering hands.

Swinging dicks smacked against my buttocks and prodded me. Roaming hands were everywhere, caressing and probing.

Fingers wedged between bodies to caress my breasts and tweak my nipples.

Harry's and Craig's fingers took liberties with my body, and I didn't mind one bit because I enjoyed every moment of the sensual teasing.

Hands found their way between my thighs, and fingers brushed over and between my slippery moist folds.

Who was exploring my pussy and rubbing my clit?

Don't know. Don't care. I can't keep track of the men and don't want to.

The skin-against-skin friction and sexiness of it all had me rubbing against them with sexy uncontrolled lusty thrusts.

Most of the time I didn't know who was touching me and whose talented fingers were bringing me to the brink—taking me to the edge until I fell over.

The physical and erotic stimulus became too much.

Calling out their names, I came hard, fast and furious in their arms.

Harry!

Craig!

Fuck! Fuck! Fuck!

I'm gonna come.

Thrusting against my husband and then against his best friend.

Rubbing my clit against their stomachs and hard dicks while they finger fucked me to ecstasy.

Biting down on the shoulder of whichever man held me at that moment.

These men knew exactly what to do with this woman's body.

"On the table," grunted a gruff voice.

What did he have in mind?

I didn't care: everything felt too damn good, and I was willing to do whatever either man wanted. I had no shame, no inhibitions, no fucking limits.

There came a point when the men couldn't hold back any longer. I honestly felt like the luckiest woman alive that they'd maintained such strength and restraint between them.

Craig carried me back to the kitchen table and laid me on it.

"I don't know whether I want to fuck you there on your back or have you bend over it," he said, thinking aloud, not asking me which I'd prefer.

And from the look of concentration on his face, I'd say he was giving his options too much thought.

He got hold of his dick and pumped it, and this was my first opportunity, so I seized it.

Laying on my side atop his kitchen table, I opened my mouth and wrapped my lips around his magnificent crown. Then, using my tongue to stroke the undercarriage, I moved my face toward him as I sucked in his length.

Slowly. Bit by bit. Enjoying the taste of his bitter-sweet precum and the sensation of my stretched opening. Thrilled by the way his dick filled my mouth and the expression on his face as he watched his cock disappear inside me.

Sucking dick is one of my favorite things to do.

I often fantasize about giving blow jobs to all the guys on the football team.

I've talked to Harry about it, and he enjoys hearing me talk about that fantasy.

I tell him how I'd like to suck all their cocks and swallow their cum.

Or perhaps they'd come all over my face, titties, and pussy.

Harry promises he'll arrange that for me one day. He'll let me become a real goo girl, and he'll get me a badge and a certificate to say how well I did at it. But I assume that's just us talking through our fantasies; it will never happen for real.

"You chose a good wife, brother." Craig moaned with pleasure.

"She's the best," my husband replied, and I could hear the pride in his voice. I loved that I made him proud. "You gonna fuck her now or later, bro?"

Later? Are we going to do this again later?

"I." Carl struggled to speak.

Thick luscious precum streamed into my mouth. His dick throbbed and twitched. He was as close to the edge as a man can get and about to lose it.

All out of staying power, he crumbled and tumbled over the fucking edge.

Grabbing a fist full of my hair, he thrust and grunted.

But who really had the upper hand here?

Me, not him. I wanted everything that had happened, and he had no chance of getting away from me without emptying into my mouth.

Not that he'd want to get away.

I wrapped one hand around his balls, and with the other, I stroked his taint. And I licked and sucked hard as if my life depended on it.

He wanted it, and so did I.

He groaned.

"Fuck. Harry. She's too good."

Salty cream oozed into my mouth; I had no intention of spilling a drop, so I kept my lips securely locked around him and sucked.

My husband was right beside us and as close as he could get without touching. Besides us, he was watching closely and tugging his length.

And I watched him from the corner of my eye.

I was sucking the cock of a dude who was practically a stranger to me. Having an attentive audience made it much more thrilling.

Hearing the little moans, sighs, and words of approval, coupled with the sight of my husband pulling his prick, only made it all even better.

Knowing what he saw turned him on.

Knowing I was doing this outrageous thing turned him on.

He was the best husband in the world to give me this gift. To have another man touch me and to let me taste another cock. To make me come so hard, so many times.

And to share this with me.

To share me with another man.

When Craig had finished fucking my throat and his dick had begun to soften, I relaxed my suction powers and let him withdraw.

Though I took hold and licked around the head to make sure he was super clean.

After that, with a wink to my husband, I opened my mouth to offer it to him, but I made sure they both saw that I hadn't completely swallowed everything.

Craig sighed: I'm sure he loved the look of his cum in my mouth as much as I liked the feeling of having it there.

If Harry was going to empty in my mouth, he had to know his jizz would mix with that of another man: his best friend from childhood. So close they were like brothers. Close enough, they were happy to share.

Shoot your cum in my mouth, husband.

But Harry had other ideas.

"Keep your mouth open, babe," he said. "But don't spill anything."

And he pumped his dick with long swift strokes launching a jetstream of white, gooey jizz across my face.

Only a little of his seed hit the target and went in my mouth. Although, perhaps my face was the real target. Either way, I was gonna insist my husband try that move again soon because being covered in cum is fucking hot.

While my husband staggered sidewards with post-orgasmic confusion and grabbed hold of the table, Craig came forward with an outstretched hand and swiped up a big gloop of my husband's sprayed seed onto his fingers, which he then placed on my bottom lip.

Of course, I leaned forward, took his fingers into my mouth, and sucked them clean like I had his cock.

If this was nudism. I could become a convert. And if it meant giving all the guys a blow job, *c'est la vie*. I'd be willing to give it a try.

"You've got yourself a hot wife, Harry," Craig said without taking his eyes off my mouth. "The guys are all gonna love her."

All in all, it left me wondering what the guys had planned for the rest of the week. I only knew Harry's older brothers were due over for lunch the next day: same house, same kitchen.

BOOK FIVE

Three-Men Prize

Feeling wholly exposed, Dee had never felt so terrified in her life.

She was nude, just like everyone else in the great hall, but they were nudists and members of this exclusive secret world; she was not. They had experience and knew what to expect, which she did not.

Ushers guided her to the small stage in the middle of the hall, where she stood facing her destiny – her prize.

Why did she ever enter that stupid competition?

The three men, James, Liam, and Cody stood tall and proud on the other side of the large padded bed.

The three kings waited for her.

Each man was king of his own domain, the elected leader, spokesman, and representative for his naturist club.

Gorgeous women and men, silent with anticipation, surrounded the stage. The audience had to be a hundred people, if not more.

They said nothing but watched her with fire in their eyes.

Under the soft lighting and the penetrating gaze of so many eyes, Dee hated to be overly proud of herself, but she was sure she looked amazing, all scrubbed clean and perfumed.

Liam stepped onto the soft pillow that separated them and offered her his hand.

Dee, following his lead, did the same and accepted his hand.

They stood facing each other, much closer, and hand in hand.

"Relax, honey," Liam whispered to her as they stood together. "I know you feel embarrassed, but this is normal. Everyone will love you."

"I'm not sure," Dee whispered back. "But I hope so. I'll do my best."

"You don't need to *do* anything special," Liam said. "All you need to do is be yourself and act on how you feel."

Then, without further explanation, Liam closed the final short distance between them and kissed Dee on the mouth.

She hummed in surprise. For a second, her body begged her to draw back—she was naked in front of strangers. Instinctively she felt like kissing should be wrong when naked and within sight of others.

But it wasn't wrong. They were there to witness her acting on instinct.

They were all naked.

She stayed the course. Slowly, her body warmed to his advance, and she kissed Liam back.

Liam did not back down from the kiss. The passion deepened. He slipped his arms around Dee's waist and drew her closer, and when he did, she felt the stirrings of his erection.

She also experienced stirrings of intimate arousal growing within herself.

Here, in front of so many sets of eyes?

HIS TONGUE SLIPPED into her mouth, and she lost all her inhibitions. It didn't matter how many people were watching—she needed him. And when his cock nudged against her stomach, she was only a little embarrassed.

Embarrassment, of course, she felt it.

Liam's thigh nudged in between Dee's, gently pushing her legs apart and pressing against the center of her arousal.

Under pressure to give her best performance, Dee was not just the guest of honor at the show. She was privileged when a hundred or more women would give anything to swap places with her on that stage.

Expecting a cold, calculating act in front of others, she experienced a genuinely passionate kiss, tender touches, and intimate excitement.

Her pussy warmed and swelled with need.

She was happy to trust in the man's leadership as long as she was in his arms, and he seemed at ease with the turn of events.

"You're stunning. You look fit for a prince or three."

"I'd hope so," Dee whispered back with a nervous giggle.

Liam's lips were back on her again, his hands slipping down to Dee's ass and squeezing as he pulled her even closer.

While she kissed him eagerly, his hard cock pressed against her. She couldn't help the moaned pleasure that escaped her lips as her moist pussy betrayed her arousal against his thigh. As soon as she heard the sound escaping from her, she heated up with embarrassment, which warmed her face.

She opened her eyes.

Behind Liam, his equal counterparts from the other clubs stood still. They watched intently, and each smiled, offering reassurance when she made eye contact. She looked them up and down and drank in the sight of two more handsome men there for her and waiting patiently to touch her. Standing still and ready for action. Their dicks stood erect, proudly saluting her.

At the sight of them, Dee's pussy throbbed.

The men stepped forward, moving closer to her.

Though Liam still held her close, the others placed their hands on her skin, on her shoulders, her back, and her ass. Cody claimed her mouth from Liam, while James kissed her neck.

She shut her eyes again lest it all became too much. She was already burning with lustful desire, and her pussy ached to be touched and filled.

Three erections pressed against her body. She wanted them all. To hold them, taste them, and come on them. To have them fill and fuck her. She'd never have believed this sort of thing would happen to her: not three men wanting to share her in an intimate but surreal way before an audience.

Hands reached between her thighs from behind, and she had no idea who, but it couldn't be Liam; his arms weren't that long.

Not a moment too soon, fingers slipped into her hungry wet slit.

Those fingers would know how ridiculously wet she was.

Soaked.

Instinctively she tried to part her legs a little wider to welcome the touch.

"I—"

Cody silenced her by intensifying their kiss.

She leaned on him as Liam pulled away and dropped to his knees before her. A moment later, she felt his hot tongue on her clit.

Flat at first and then moving; hot and damp; warm breath.

Conscious of the position of all her men, she realized it must have been James's fingers inside her. They still teased, moving slowly, keeping her turned on but not giving enough to make her come.

With Liam's tongue in action, everything changed, and an orgasm was imminent.

But James was behind her, and Dee moaned with great surprise when his tongue delved into the cleft of her ass.

She rapidly approached the edge of orgasm and was damn sure it would just be the first of many.

Cody broke off their kiss to whisper in her ear. "Bend over, my princess. Let James fuck you from behind now. I will hold you steady, and you can hold on to me."

She let her hand slide down his muscular arms to rest near his elbows. She sensed impressive strength there.

He stepped back a little and lowered his arms. She bent over.

Liam adapted his position to continue his oral administration to her labia and clit.

Her loose breasts swung freely below her, and she became self-consciously aware of gravity pulling on her bullet-hard nipples.

Her mouth was at the same height as Cody's cock. A glistening pool of precum topped its swollen head and looked too good to ignore.

In her peripheral vision, she saw those gathered had moved together in couples and small groups and also touched each other. For the first time, she glanced to the side to properly gauge the reactions of the others. The audience had begun to kiss and touch, too.

Some continued to watch them; others paid more attention to the people they stood with.

Bodies met bodies.

Soon, Dee wasn't the only one moaning. She felt more at ease knowing she and the three kings weren't the only ones aroused and weren't being watched by a stoic audience.

The fingers left her passage, and the tongue that had licked around and in her ass moved away.

She sensed the man rising to his feet and standing behind her before he rubbed the end of his cock along the crack of her ass.

Was James going to fuck her ass?

The idea both shocked and excited her. She knew in an instant that if he asked, she'd consent.

Unable to resist, she lapped at the head of Cody's cock in front of her. The sticky precum tasted like sweet nectar. She licked her tongue around it. And it was all the more delicious knowing people watched her do this.

Behind her, James pushed his cock further down and nudged her wet entrance. She almost felt disappointed that he'd gone south of her asshole. He leaned over her, his body hot against her back. And he said, "Will you take it? Will you take my seed inside and let me breed you?"

It sounded so crude and daring.

Something they should have discussed before. Not the question to be asked in front of an audience.

"Yes," she said, "anything. Do anything." And she meant it. She was there for them to do whatever they fucking liked; that was always the plan. That was what she'd agreed to. She'd even signed a contract.

Her clit throbbed so hard. She was about to come, no matter what.

James said, "I want to show you off to every single person in this room. For them to see you and know you are the chosen one."

The chosen winner.

One of Liam's hands moved up Dee's chest and tweaked her nipple.

"Do it. Fuck me," she begged. She wanted the leaders of each community to show her and everyone exactly what he'd just said. Dee felt proud at that moment.

Her cheeks heated, and she knew she should be embarrassed, but she couldn't bring herself to care. The surrounding crowds kissed and groped and—now and then—turned their heads to watch the three perform with the woman *they'd* chosen for the ceremonial orgy.

It was hot as hell that people were watching and getting aroused while doing so.

With her nudity, her arousal, and her lovers, she was bringing a whole room of people to their knees—her pleasure meant their pleasure.

Dee wanted to put on a show as much as the guys wanted to give it.

James entered her with ease just when it was impossible for her to hold on. She thrust back against his cock. He pushed forward into her, pushing her clit against Liam's tongue. She had to let Cody's cock drop from her mouth in order both to breathe and cry out in ecstasy.

She came.

And came.

But Cody's cock was delicious, and she wanted to connect with him and the other two men, so she continued to lick around the glans through her cries and the contractions of her gratification.

Mercilessly, James didn't stop thrusting, and she didn't want him to.

For a while, she was out of sorts, delirious.

Her body only came to rest at the first plateau, and she had no doubt more orgasms would follow.

They did.

Before Dee knew it, she lay on the soft stage she'd previously stood on. James's body on top of hers. The other men were next to her on either side and cuddling her. The kissing continued. One man and then another claimed her mouth. Their hands were all over her. Every touch was blissful on her skin.

Everything hotter than she'd ever known before.

Dee stole a glance around the room. It confirmed they were doing this in front of others. There were still a few people watching them. Others in the audience had tumbled to the floor in each other's arms.

James's cock was in her again. He hadn't come yet, not one of the three expert lovers had come. They exercised exemplary self-control while giving her untold pleasure.

She was ready. She was prepared to come again, helped by the fact that each thrust into her involved his body rubbing against her swollen clit. Helped because she had two hot guys on either side of her, covering her with kisses. But all she wanted was for them to take turns fucking her in every position and every orifice.

Having never been with multiple men at a time before, and having never fucked as part of a stage show, now she had the opportunity it seemed a shame that there wasn't a cock in her mouth and one in her cunt. And she entertained curious thoughts about the logistics of double penetration too.

JAMES QUICKENED THE pace. Thrusting deep. Deep growls seemed to come from somewhere within him. "Join us, fellas," he said. "We should come together."

The men on either side of her got up onto their knees.

Their cocks bobbed above her.

She looked at them, and all three sets of eyes focused on her—all dark with lust.

"Are you all right, Dee?" James asked.

"Yes, please, fill me, breed me," she said. And looking at the three men, without thinking about the other people in the room, she added, "Cover me with your cum."

It was all the consent and encouragement the men needed. She couldn't be sure who came first. The hot flood within her came at the same time spurts of white goo crisscrossed her body and splattered over her.

It was the most outrageous thing Dee had ever done, and she loved it.

From somewhere, Cody produced damp cloths. He handed one each to his accomplices, and they wiped her clean.

A glance about the room confirmed they were at the center of an orgy: their fucking inspiring countless other bodies to seek pleasure and satisfaction.

"I want to fuck you," Liam whispered.

"As do I," Cody said.

"I'd like to know that our seed mixed within you." James seemed remarkably composed.

The men cuddled her, stroked her, and kissed her until they were all rock hard again, and Dee was ready for more.

Cody parted Dee's legs, pushing her knees up and bent so that her feet were flat on the floor to support the weight of her legs.

And his head went down.

The familiar sensation of the warm tongue flattening and dancing over her clit and between her slit made Dee's channel flood with desire and natural lubricant.

On impulse, Dee raised her ass, pushing upward, and Cody filled her with his fingers.

"Let me suck your cock, please," she begged Liam as she hadn't paid him enough attention yet.

She couldn't imagine anything better than being fingered by one stranger while giving head to another. And that was what these men were to her. They'd never met until they came together on that stage. She'd seen only photographs of the men.

The men had chosen her.

They'd picked her from however many contestants entered that competition, which they ran over social media. It was easy and free to enter by sending a few photos and answering some simple questions.

At the time, Dee had no idea what she was entering, but an all-expenses naturist break sounded like an appealing prize when Dee had no idea what that entailed. The event organizer arranged everything, and an army of capable women prepared her that day with massages, grooming, and pep talks.

Everything in her life brought her to the night when she was the star of a live sex show, and her fellow performers were strangers to her.

"You want my cock in your pretty mouth? Of course, I'm happy to oblige," Liam replied, calm and confident. His expression was almost a sneer.

She turned her head to one side. Although she was lying down, her head was propped on more pillows.

He knelt beside her head and fed her his long shaft.

She couldn't take it all. She looked up at him. Even like this, he seemed the sure-of-himself dominant male who took control. She liked the experience of him and his fellow club leaders using her.

The satisfaction was mutual.

They'd all made a point of gaining her consent. Even so, she had a weakness for cocky bastards. These three fitted the bill, especially Liam, who had haughty arrogance off to a fine art. And why not? He was stunning to look at.

"This is what you want," Liam spoke in a sultry voice.

Where Liam was audacious, Cody was sweet and tender. James simply projected the confidence of the man who could be King of the Fucking World if he wanted to be.

From her other side, James whispered, "We all know what you want. Your desires are like an open book to us, and we share them."

Cody's tongue flicked over Dee's clit.

They knew what she wanted, a fact she found so erotic.

"We're a perfect match." Liam leaned in a little closer. His cock filled her mouth just a little beyond what was comfortable. She was almost gagging. But not quite.

It was incredible.

Dee whimpered, not even sure what Liam was referring to, but yes. It was probably true. They were three strangers who wanted to do this with her, and she wanted it too, which made them well-matched.

When he withdrew his cock completely, she said, "Oh, yes."

And she felt it.

Just, yes.

It seemed that Dee's soul was happy to share her innermost private fantasies with these strangers and act them out for real.

There was no fighting it. Why should she? Dee was coming undone, and the strange men knew all her buttons and exactly how to press them.

Fucking her in every way in front of a crowd of strangers, Dee would usually prefer not to comment.

"Liam," Dee moaned. She looked up at Liam. "Oh god…"

She tried to stay still and let Cody take complete control, but she couldn't stop writhing with pleasure.

Forcefully, he took charge. With a self-assured assertiveness, he thrust his cock into her, watching her with a grin on his face. When Dee gasped, Liam pushed his cock into her mouth. James's fingers were on her asshole and close to breaching the tight hole.

Life could get no better than it was there and then.

Cody fucked her hard and deep in a way that reached those parts and was just so fucking right.

On the outskirts of the room, Dee heard skin slapping against skin and moans becoming louder.

More of the others also engaged in uninhibited sex, no longer bothered about being an attentive audience.

Some hungry eyes still devoured her while they focused on the staged show. She felt their gaze and their greed. She knew all the things the men were doing to her were making those on the outskirts of the room hot and turned on.

She was inspiring a room full of strangers.

Wanton and debauched.

Like something from her most private fantasies.

Dee loved it.

She wanted them to see.

She wanted all of them to see her fucked by three men.

To see her take pleasure in that way like as if she deserved it.

She bucked her hips and gasped.

Hands were all over her.

Fingers teased her nipples.

Fingers stroked her ass cheeks and her asshole.

"Come for me. Don't hold back. Let them see how good we are together," Cody instructed.

"You're so good," Liam praised.

James's cock rubbed against the crack of her ass but didn't enter. "You're doing so well. Lead them, sweet girl. Lead them into pleasure. They adore you. I adore you."

Dee blinked back tears. This was her doing—she was the purpose behind the ceremonial show and the driving force behind each orgasm about to happen in that great hall.

Her.

Taking a shuddering breath, she was already shaking from pleasure and the thrill of the exhibition.

She did as requested.

Without shame or inhibition, she cried out loudly as one orgasm after another pulsed through her. Wave after wave of euphoria washed over her, taking her higher to an ultimate climax.

She felt powerful—there was power in being desired. Dee loved the attention. She hoped to live in the perverted fantasies of the audience for a long time.

Having come inside her, Cody pulled out.

Snapping back to reality, Dee gasped. She missed the fullness, but there were two other men besides her with hard cocks aching for satisfaction.

Where one man left a space, another was nearby and ready to step in and fill it. Sort of.

James helped Dee get on her hands and knees for him, which allowed him easier access to her rear. He had already shown he was a butt man, this time, he went down on her ass and smooched it in a way she'd never experienced before. It was warm and wet and set every nerve-ending tingling. Her tight star relaxed and opened for him. She couldn't fight it if she tried. She wanted him in there.

She let him in: tongue, fingers, and then his big fat cock buried into her ass and fucked her like it was her pussy. He wasn't slow and gentle, and she didn't want him to be.

They were tuning in to baser instincts and primitive needs. The need to fuck and be fucked.

"Fuck me. Fuck, yes. Fuck me filthy. Ruin me." She murmured many obscenities under her breath. She wouldn't last many strokes without coming hard with a dick in her a-hole.

Someone grabbed her hair and pulled it.

Pulled her head back. And a thick cock bounced against her lips.

"You want to suck this, babe? Or something else?"

She opened her mouth, and the next thrust in her ass pushed her forward to engulf Liam's dick.

It was enough. Too much. She thrust her ass back against James, and he worked hard into her as they came together.

Without giving her any time to recover, the guys bumped fists and changed places.

James sat back. He had time to watch and recover. But Liam didn't give her a minute before he slipped inside her cunt, where Cody's spunk must have added to the juiciness.

He held onto her hair again, pulling it hard enough to make her know it but not enough to hurt badly. Fucking perfect.

Her first public shag fest might last for hours. Her first, but hopefully not her last.

BOOK SIX

Taken by the Tattooed Biker

I WAS RAISED IN A FAMILY of naturists, so our away-from-home breaks were typically textile-free in a campsite somewhere warm. We always have a lot of fun together, but on one particular trip, I kept finding myself unusually hot and bothered, and it wasn't because of the weather.

A large group of bikers pitched up next to us. They looked scary and fierce when they descended on the area like a menacing gang all dressed in big boots and head to toe in black leathers. But that would change.

Going nude generally brings about remarkable equality as we're all equally human and vulnerable without our armor or expensive costumes.

And the biker guys and girls turned out to be as friendly as teddy bears and as cute as kittens. They weren't one of those outlaw biker gangs that make the news headlines; they were a group of enthusiastic nudists who also enjoyed something fast and powerful throbbing between their thighs.

The problem for me was many of the biker men were as hot as chocolate croissants straight from the oven and just as sweet.

When they weren't dressed in black leather, they were muscles on muscles, rippling abs, and all inked up with colorful images, tribal patterns, and plain writing.

I wanted to stare at them but knew it was bad manners. I wanted to get closer and study the ink, and I wanted to examine more than just the tattoos.

The jewelry that adorned their bodies also caught my attention. Not just earrings and finger rings but pierced nipples, tummy buttons, and curious flashes of silver lower down too. I wanted to investigate those genital piercings close up, but would I ever get the opportunity?

To a horny teenage girl like myself, the biker guys were sex on legs. They looked like gods and flirted like demons. If anyone of them sent out an open invitation to his bed, I'd go.

I should be more discerning, but you only live once.

And if you can't be discerning, then be discreet.

Discretion is difficult in a tent in the middle of a busy camping field. I was with my large family, but at eighteen, I was old enough to have my own tent and didn't have to sleep in my parent's campervan.

When a male voice whispered outside my tent at night and asked me if I fancied a moonlit walk down to the lake, I was out of the door before I realized who it was.

And thrilled to discover the voice belonged to Logan.

He smelled good and turned me on.

I had no reason to feel guilty.

What did he ask?

Will you come with me?

That was it. I wanted to *come* with him more than he knew.

I was single and old enough. If I wanted to do things by the lake or in the woods that we had to pass on the way to the water's edge with a stranger, then I could make that decision.

"Will you come with me?" he repeated.

He wore nothing on his upper body except a sleeveless denim cut and no t-shirt. Tribal tattoos snaked around both his arms. His washboard abs and small silver hoops through his nipples were right there on display, but blue denim jeans covered his legs. He must have thought it chilly in the dark.

My nipples were hardening under the cool night air, but he kept his eyes on my face.

It's not unusual for nudists to wear clothes when practical; lots of people think we stay naked regardless of the weather, but we aren't crazy.

"Give me one minute." I dashed back inside and pulled on a maxi dress, plus thick socks and sensible walking shoes.

HE HELD ON TO MY HAND, our fingers entwined, while we walked quietly through the campsite. It was late, but not that late. Many people hadn't gone to sleep yet and were sitting outside and having hushed conversations.

We were soon at the perimeter, away from the tents, caravans, and campervans; we passed through the small gate onto the footpath that led to the lake.

The full moon kept the path well-lit; an open meadow lay on one side where a hunting fox stalked its prey, an owl hooted somewhere in the forest on the other.

The long dark shadows didn't encourage conversation, and we still didn't speak. It seemed a crime to break into the sound of nature doing whatever it did at night.

After a few minutes, we were halfway to the lake when he stopped walking and pulled me to halt beside him.

I looked up into his kind face. His stubble looked soft, and I wanted to stroke his chin, but I didn't think we were at that stage yet, and he still held one of my hands.

On the other hand, he did seem to think we were at that stage. He stroked the back of his fingers along my jawline, bringing them to rest on my chin. He tilted my face upward. I held my breath, anticipating a kiss.

His lips brushed close to mine, they barely touched.

The feather-light contact set my heart racing - banging so loud he must have heard it - and butterflies fluttering in my stomach. My entire body reacted and pure lust pulsed through my veins.

When he dropped his hand from my face, stepped back, and released his grip on my other hand, I glanced away from his penetrating gaze in order to catch a breath.

I looked down at the mysterious inky script crossing his chest near his nipple ring.

Then I noticed the bulging crotch of his jeans.

My private parts were equally aflame.

We were a couple of hundred feet from the campsite and barely out of hearing range, and my clothes peeled away in the experienced, masterful hands of the man. It didn't take a lot of skill to slip the straps from my shoulder and let the dress fall to the ground, which left me completely exposed to his hungry gaze as I hadn't bothered with underwear.

Of course he'd seen my body before, but did he always look at me in that way? Perhaps he did in his mind, I hadn't noticed him doing so.

But I'd certainly ogled him enough to know about the metal jewelry adorning his dick. I'd looked it up on the internet to discover it was a Prince Albert.

He brushed his hands gently over my breasts before squeezing them firmly, making me gasp. He lowered himself to flick his tongue over my hard nipples, which sent my head spinning.

He licked and then closed his teeth down, a bite hard enough to pinch but not seriously hurt. As he only had one mouth, but I had two boobies, he pinched my other nipple and rolled it between his fingers.

It made me weak at the knees, which was his cue to sweep me off my feet. He lifted me as if I were weightless and lowered me onto the soft mossy bed that lay between the path and the forest.

I propped myself on my elbows and watched him tackle my sturdy, laced footwear.

Logan stroked the bare skin of my legs, over my shins, knees, and thighs, until a palm sank down over my crotch as if he owned it.

His hand moved over the mound and pressed with greater pressure until his fingers slipped between the delicate folds of skin.

My arousal lubricated the motion making it smooth and easy.

With a gasp, I tilted my hips, rubbing myself against him.

Urging him on.

It was all new to me. I'd never been touched in quite this way by anyone before, and I never expected to be handled so slowly and with such reverence. The gentleness of his touches, the way he seemed to worship me, was in sharp contrast to his aggressive biker-gang appearance.

I never expected such an experience with a stranger.

Yet, without apprehension, caution, or shame, I didn't attempt to stop him. My body. My Choice. My desires. I submitted.

My head fell back, and I spread my legs wider, showing him all I had to offer — inviting his touch. Eager for his cock. I wanted him to fuck me more than anything else right there and then.

It didn't seem like he were a stranger.

His caresses made me hold my breath in anticipation of what would follow, as if my breathing might change his course of action.

His fingers sank deeper into the wet heat, but not deep enough. Not penetrating in the way I wanted but turning me on and getting me worked up without scratching the itch and hitting the spot.

Ever sure of himself, Logan's hands coaxed noises from me. Embarrassing squeaks and sighs that I didn't intend to share. Still, his palm held steady and firm against my swollen clit. All of his attention was on me. Providing me with pleasure. Wringing gratifying moans from my mouth.

The sensation overwhelmed me, and I'd never been so aroused before.

His fingers slipped around my self-lubricated folds and easily inside her dripping wet channel. I don't think I'd ever been so wet before nor more eager to come. I'd never experienced such uninhibited freedom with a stranger in an unfamiliar outdoor place.

"Logan." I gasped while writhing in pleasure. "Oh my God."

"Shh..." He smiled before lowering his face out of view to apply his tongue to the place places his fingers had already visited.

I wanted to watch him, which conflicted with the urge to shut my eyes tightly. More than anything, though, I wanted him to enter me. To fuck me. To hit all those pleasant spots inside and make me come.

Condoms?

The thought drifted through my mind.

Perhaps he has some. Men carried stuff like that, didn't they? I didn't.

If the worst came to the worst, there was the morning-after pill. I certainly didn't want to stop.

I didn't want to make important decisions.

He took control like he owned my body and knew how to treat it. I had no complaints because I had no idea a mouth could deliver such divine bliss. His tongue dipped between each fold and worked up and down from my clit to my ass.

At the same time, a finger or two slipped easily inside my tight virginal pussy.

I was losing control and about to come any moment, but I didn't want this joy to ever end.

Right then, I'd do anything, but Logan asked for nothing. The man only gave and gave and gave with his tongue, his mouth, and his fingers.

Breathless and silent, I panted and gasped as Logan held me on the edge of ecstasy.

I longed for more, wanted to touch him, to know him as he knew me. But he rendered me helpless. I'd never needed something or someone so much in my life. It was ridiculous because I didn't even know him beyond his name and his motorcycle.

Unfamiliar emotions surged and threatened to engulf me. I didn't understand them.

I worked my hips in slow, desperate motions. And called out, "Logan! Oh, Logan!"

The pleasure didn't stop. Wantonly, I spread my legs a little and thrust my crotch forward against his face, encouraging his hot and wet tongue to continue as it had: firm and soft, giving and exploring.

He responded to my body, fucking with his fingers harder and deeper.

Such never-known pleasure became too much to bear.

After timeless minutes of willing endurance, I succumbed to the inescapable pleasure. Each new touch became explosive. I couldn't imagine anything as good again.

I sucked in a breath. Tears fell down my cheeks as I strained her head upward, and my entire body clenched tight and tense.

Bliss incarnate took hold. Parts of my body that I never knew existed tingled and sparked with joy.

"Logan." His name was the only word I could say.

"My Lucy," he whispered in return.

Lost to pleasure, I wanted as much as he could give, and he showed no sign of stopping. Playing my body, taking me on.

Eventually, I raised a weak hand in protest. "No more, please, no more," I begged him to stop.

He stilled his movement instantly on request and changed positions to lay down beside me, wrapping his large body around mine.

The alien harshness of his denim jeans and belt buckle came as a jolt. How selfishly I'd enjoyed his touch when he remained dressed.

I didn't have time to ponder or act on that thought as I sensed his arms moving. A clank followed by the swish of leather as he undid the belt and then the popping sound as he unbuttoned his fly.

He arched his back and pushed his jeans away.

I barely registered his massive erection with glinting metal additions when he rolled me over onto my side, facing away from him.

I hadn't expected that.

He held me, and behind me, he adjusted himself. His huge shaft slipped against my ass.

Does he want to fuck my ass?

Against my buttocks, I felt the sticky moisture of his precum, the hardness of his huge dick, and something oddly more solid.

My clit tingled as I thought about the shiny metal that pierced his dick.

His breath labored behind me while I felt his hand on my ass as he handled his dick, maneuvering it to nestle between my thighs.

He thrust a couple of long, slow movements back and forth into the space, rubbing against me rather than penetrating me. Near the entrance but not in it

His thick, hard member felt incredible and erotic between my legs as he fucked my thighs. Solid warm metal and a hard warm cock slipped in and out of that space.

An act so intimate and erotic. I never knew it was possible, but from the way he moved, grinding against me, and from his shallow breaths, I knew he liked it.

And me? He's satisfied me already, and I wouldn't prevent him from using my body in any way he pleased.

I'd expected him to enter and fuck me and never considered that a man might derive pleasure in any other way.

But this? *This* was so erotic. Him rubbing against me and fucking my thighs was unheard of—sex without penetration. And I felt thoroughly used and loved it.

What other new things can he show me? How much more can this older man teach me?

After a few long strokes, he wrapped a long arm around me and placed his hand on my clit.

"No, I can't take anymore." I covered his hand with mine. "Not there. But I'd like you in me. I want you to fuck me." I wanted him to know it was all right and he had my full consent.

I wanted to share the ultimate experience with him.

He moaned, and loud incomprehensible words fell from his lips.

He might've been swearing in a foreign language, as I understood not one word of it.

At the same time, he moved his hand to my hips and continued to jerk his body. His thrusts became faster and more furious—his breathing: less controlled.

He was losing control.

I stayed as still as possible, enjoying him and allowing him to use my body.

Knowing I turned him on so much and got him so worked up thrilled me.

His lips met the back of my neck. He kissed with an open mouth, biting and sucking passionately.

His thrusts gained speed as he moved between my accommodating thighs.

I pressed back against him.

His body shuddered and fell still, and at that instant, I felt warmth between my legs as his cum flooded out. It quickly began to cool and to dribble around and down because gravity didn't stop working.

If we had been in a bed, we might have fallen asleep in each other's arms. But the reality of the dark world around us returned all too quickly.

I pulled my dress from beneath me and used it to wipe up the sticky mess on my legs. I might never wash that dress again but keep it.

Logan's arms wrapped around me and held me firmly in place. "Just one more minute," he muttered. But one more minute and we might fall asleep.

Neither of us wanted to move.

We must.

I'd gone ahead and offered myself to an older man who I barely knew.

And I didn't feel guilt, fear, or shame—only satisfaction.

He'd used me exactly how he wanted, but did it mean I was still a virgin after all that?

He pulled me to my feet, and only then did he realize my dress was sticky and wet as I used it for the cleanup, and I had nothing to wear.

"It's not a problem. I'm not cold, and we don't have far to walk back."

"You can wear my denim?"

I shook my head. "No, it's too big and looks better on you. Really, I'm fine," I insisted. "But you can get dressed," while I retie my shoelaces.

"It's easier than carrying my clothes," he said.

"And you look sexy in your clothes," I encouraged him to get dressed largely for my ulterior motives.

Being naked but in the company of a sexy man who was clothed was my own particular kink.

BOOK SEVEN
Naked Guesthouse

Welcome to my naturist B&B, which welcomes travelers who seek us out as a destination as well as those who are passing through the area on business. It never hurts to mix business and pleasure.

As the proprietor of The Forest Garden B&B, I'm dedicated to providing the best possible experience. And many people visit us time and time again after discovering the personalized service and attention to detail that I'm able to provide.

Many of our guests don't live the nudist lifestyle on a full-time basis, so the opportunity to relax and let it all hang out here without fear of judgment is a real selling point.

I'm an open-minded woman who truly enjoys the company of men. And I go above and beyond to ensure that each and every guest has a stay that exceeds their expectations. I run the place as much as a passion-project hobby as to pay the bills.

For the business traveler seeking female companionship and relaxation, I endeavor to meet their needs. In addition to conversation and companionship, I also offer a wonderful, relaxing full-body massage.

Whatever they need, I'm happy to do it, and with nothing on, because this is a naturist establishment.

On top of everything else, we also serve up the best home-cooked food with the knowledge that the way to a man's heart is through his stomach. My husband is a chef who trained in the very best kitchens before bringing his culinary skills closer to home.

Now, I may have given you the wrong impression. I am not offering a lusty woman with every breakfast, I am not a prostitute! In fact, sexual services of any kind aren't for sale here.

The easiest way to explain how things work here is for me to tell you a story or two about a typical day at work for me.

Yesterday, Mr. Jarrow, Jerry, booked an evening massage session to help him unwind after his long journey. He wanted a one-hour, full-body massage, which was charged to his room at the local rate.

We went out to the therapy studio. I call it the studio; it's a beautifully appointed back garden shed. It looks like a colorful cabin from the outside, but it's warm and cozy inside with soft mood lighting and the subtle scent of lavender essential oil. And it's all set up for relaxing massage treatments.

I started massaging his back, and when the massage was complete, sixty minutes later, he was lying on his back with an erection like a tent pole. I'd done nothing to provoke his penis in that way.

Except we were both naked, and I'd been stroking my hands all over his body. And my boobs are on the large side, so when I reached across him at times, my boobs rubbed over him too.

Look, relaxing like that just feels nice, and sometimes men get hard. Okay, my clients usually get erections.

Mr. Jarrow's was an extensive statement of arousal. It was about average girth but longer than most, and I couldn't help wondering how much I would be able to fit in my mouth.

Can you blame me? You'd also be wondering the same thing if you saw it.

And my pussy was wet and swollen with excitement after spending an hour with my hands on his extremely fit body. I'm only human!

Seeing him in that state was more than I needed to get me turned on too. I wanted to feel a big cock like his inside me but not there and then in that relaxing space. I never have penetrative intercourse in the massage studio; instead, I prefer to practice self-control and wait.

"The massage has come to an end," I said. "I can leave you to relax, but I'd be happy to suck your cock now if you'd like."

I wanted to suck it.

I wanted to taste it and touch it. So I asked if I could.

Oral sex is not on the menu to order at the B&B, and the guests don't pay for it. I just do it if I want to and if they are willing. And I'll let you know a secret, I usually want to, and they're usually willing.

I just love sucking cocks. I love it about as much as I love having cum in my mouth. And I also love being surrounded by men who cover my tits in cum.

So, I know what I like, and life is too short to miss out, so if I can, I'll go for it.

Like I did with Mr. Jarrow.

"Yes, please," he whispered.

Lowering my head, I slowly swirled my tongue around and across the crown. It bounced about while I groaned with delight at the sweet taste of his precum on the tip of my tongue.

I licked down the length of his shaft with my tongue. And when I reached the root, I licked all the way back to the end of his rock-hard dick.

It was as stiff as a broom handle.

Sensing that he was nearing the edge of self-control, I opened my mouth wide and slowly lowered it over his shaft.

Only a few bobbing movements later, he shot his cum into the back of my mouth. There was so much, and it kept pumping.

I kept my head going up and down like a piston, sucking his large cock, but I couldn't swallow all of his cum fast enough; it soon filled my mouth and began to dribble out.

A considerable amount of cum dribbled down my chin despite my best effort to keep us clean. I swiped at the mess on my chin with my fingers and proceeded to lick them clean.

After Jerry had stopped pumping and looked serenely blissed out, I told him to relax for as long as he wanted; I wrapped him in warm fluffy towels and assured him I'd be back to wake him if he fell asleep on the heated massage couch. After all, he'd paid for a very comfortable bed in a nice room with an ensuite.

Apart from the sandals on my feet, I was completely naked, but it would take a long cold shower to cool me down. I was extremely turned on after seeing and tasting Mr. Jarrow's erection. If I thought that was the end of everything, I would've been frustrated, but I was confident there'd be more fun to come that evening.

I walked across the garden to enter the guesthouse through the sunroom, where Michael and Larry were sitting, talking, and enjoying the view. They greeted me with friendly smiles, and I told them I wanted to shower before joining them.

I wanted to be happy and fulfilled in my work, so I set up a naturist B&B with a twist, and it allowed me to meet like-minded clients who became my friends: men like Larry and my husband, Michael.

The public area had an open-plan layout. The communal shower was between the hot tub and the steam room and in plain view of Michael and Larry.

The men continued talking while they both turned to watch me soaping myself up. I was so hot and horny that an interested male audience was welcome, but I didn't want to linger under the wet jets when they probably planned something much dirtier.

My feet were wide apart, allowing the tepid water to wash over my nether regions. It also ensured my audience had a clear view of the flow of clean water dripping from around that area. I hoped they enjoyed the soapy shower show.

I turned off the jet and grabbed a fresh towel from the pile.

After patting myself to remove some of the moisture, I wandered over to the guys. "It was hot in the massage room," I declared as I continued to towel myself dry.

Larry chuckled. "As always."

"It's getting warmer in here, too." My husband let the towel slip away from his lap, revealing a growing hard on. "Are you going to join us now?"

I glanced at Larry. While looking at my face, he also pushed his towel aside to reveal an eager cock stretching out for attention.

The guys were well aware of what they were doing to me.

As I was still standing in front of them with my crotch almost level with their faces, I raised one leg and rested my foot up on a chair to ensure they both had an excellent view of my swollen, protruding pussy lips.

Using my fingertips, I stroked around my swollen clit and the length of my moist folds. All the time, I continued watching the men who were watching me. Their focus had slipped from my face to my pussy lips.

All three of us enjoyed anticipating what might follow.

"I think we'd all like some fun," I said after a few minutes.

"I'd like to see Larry lick you," said Michael.

"Only if you want to," I added, looking at Larry.

He seemed pleased with the suggestion and lost no time getting to his knees in front of me. I did not move; I continued standing with one foot on the floor and the other on a chair so his tongue could easily access my lady parts.

Despite being a man of few words, Larry was a wonderful tease with his skillful tongue and mouth.

Slowly and gently, he breathed on my mound and barely touched me with the soft, moist tip of his tongue. When I was almost ready to beg for more, he licked me firmly but all too briefly. Pushing me close to the climax but not close enough.

Next, the tongue probed the folds of flesh, and perhaps there were fingers too; it was hard to tell as I was so wet, and it was all painfully gentle. I wanted more: firmer, harder, just more.

While I experienced this pleasurable soft torture, I stared at Michael, and he stared right back at me. Reclining in his chair, he appeared very comfortable, like he was enjoying the show.

Larry was sucking my clit and fingering me: do you have any idea how good it felt? I held the top of his head with one hand, but only very gently because I didn't want to distract him from the excellent performance.

My other hand squeezed one of my breasts.

There is only so much pleasure a woman can take in a standing position before her knees go weak and give way.

"Enough!" I gently pulled Larry away from my soaking wet, throbbing pussy by his hair. "Enough of that. It must be my turn now."

He stood up, and I sank to my knees in front of him.

Precum dripped from his fat hard cock, which I always find incredibly sexy.

Opening my mouth wide, I held my head back and shuffled under him so that any dribbles from his dick would fall directly into my mouth.

He looked down at me, and I looked up at him. And the eye contact was electric.

I raised to lick the bulbous crown of his magnificent cock. Swiping my tongue over the tip, I lapped up every drop of the delicious pooling precum. The taste of him made my clit throb harder; it was a potent aphrodisiac.

From the corner of my eye, I saw Michael stroking his own dick and watching intensely; he enjoyed watching me with other men as much as I enjoyed it: we were lucky to find each other so compatible in our quirks.

My tongue continued to dance around Larry's cock, teasing and pleasing him and enjoying the taste of his leaking tip.

After a few minutes, there was a second hard dick in front of my face. Michael had stood up to join in the fun.

Don't worry, Michael; I had NO intention of leaving you out.

Taking both men in hand, I'd hold on to one cock while entertaining the other with my mouth, and I switched back and forth between the two. You may have seen two dicks sharing a woman's mouth and face in porn. I'm here to tell you, as the woman, it's dead hot in real life.

My own juices made my crotch all sticky, and wet ran and ran down my legs; I was so turned on.

But I didn't touch my ladyparts because my hands were occupied; I held on to their dicks and fondled their balls. I had my hands full - and my face full - but knew my turn would come again soon enough. And after swapping my mouth from one to the other for a while, I decided it was time to get off my knees and change things around.

Michael moved behind me, standing close enough that I could feel his erection pushing into my lower back. The heat from his cock warmed my skin, which made me shiver pleasurably.

We needed no words to choreograph the dance as I led the men to a more comfortable place in the room, a massive couch that could accommodate three adults or more.

If they wanted me to take either one of their big cocks deep inside me, then it might be wise to have a large padded surface to play on.

I wasn't going to disappoint them. The guys shoved me onto the sofa and placed themselves on either side of me, so they had full access to every part of my willing body.

They worked together to turn me on more with their caresses and prise my thighs apart.

Larry started at my shoulders, slowly moving down to my neck and my breasts.

Michael reached forward to cup one of my boobs and gave a gentle squeeze, but hard enough to make me moan softly. He played his fingers over my nipple and gently tweaked it, knowing perfectly well the effect it would have on me.

It felt wonderful. I closed my eyes briefly to savored the experience via my other sences.

When Larry got to my stomach, he paused. He kissed his way up my ribcage paying extra attention to my nipples on the way up to my neck.

I turned my head toward Michael, and our lips met in a tender kiss. And while we were distracted, Larry got down between my thighs and began eating me out.

Without breaking our kiss, I was aware that Michael was also aware of what Larry was getting up to, or should I say, going down?

I would never complain about anyone going down on me, but I was so horny and wanted more.

"Which one of you is going to fuck me first?" I asked.

Bless him, Larry raised a hand but didn't take his face away from my pussy to actually answer. I liked his persistence and commitment to the job. I had pushed his head away with a gentle shove, or else he'd never stop. And I turned over onto my knees.

My pussy needed pounding, and I knew that would be the best position to receive the hard fucking I desired.

Before long, I was on my knees, sucking Larry with Michael fucking me.

I can't tell you how much I needed his big dick to fill me and how good each thrust felt when he entered, and his balls slapped against me. I was in the perfect position for him to hit all the right spots.

Michael held on tightly to me. He had to while I bucked and writhed; I was determined to get as much as possible from the position. It felt fucking fantastic, and I soon lost all self-control.

Larry's cock fell from my mouth when I needed my airways clear so as to call out and moan with satisfaction as I came like a volcano letting off steam.

I wouldn't have minded if Larry had jerked his cock and covered my face with his cum right then: I love that sort of thing.

I love everything about spunk: eating it, the look, the smell, and being covered in spunk. Take my picture!

Larry did none of that; he's too much of a gentleman.

And both of these gents had magnificent self-control.

After a while — and multiple orgasms for me — we switched positions, by which I mean I stayed in the middle, and they swapped.

We were enjoying every moment, every stroke.

We were all at the edge of orgasm but holding back as if we were on a movie set, waiting for the director to shout, "CUM!"

I became aware that we were being watched.

It took a while to notice the voyeur; with the lighting being brighter in the room than outside, he was hidden, and I had no idea how long he'd been out there and watching us.

Larry and Michael were performing like porn stars, so they may have also noticed the figure standing outside and looking in through the window with his dick in his hand. Having an audience may have spurred on their performance.

Of course the voyeur was another guest, my massage client, on his way in from the studio. He'd become caught up in our little performance. There are TVs in the guest rooms, but we were giving him something else to watch.

I wondered if he might prefer to join in or whether he preferred to watch from a distance.

Of course, I had to slow things down with Larry and Michael in order to call out and invite him to join us. But that's just the sacrifice I am willing to make as a caring business owner who goes above and beyond to ensure that an overnight stay will exceed the expectation of my guests.

Mr. Jarrow shook his head and stepped back into the evening shadows, and we kept him in mind when we went for our grand finale.

My pussy had received the seeing to that I wanted – several times over. So I got on my knees and took the two men in hand.

"Let's start as we mean to finish. I mean, finish as we started," I garbled out my message, but they seemed to understand.

They both rubbed their leaking dicks over my face, my lips, my cheeks while my tongue darted about. One then the other dipped his dick in my mouth all too briefly, and they began to tug their dicks with speed and expertise.

We all knew what was coming.

One white ribbon of cum followed another as they splattered over my face. My mouth was wide open, and some when inside but capturing it all in my mouth was never the point. The point was a good time was had by all including me.

When they'd come, the men allowed me to lick their dicks completely clean, and only after that did I clean myself down.

Somehow, Mr. Jarrow slipped quietly away, and I didn't see him until I went to check on him in his room with his personal early morning wake-up call the next day.

BOOK EIGHT

Teacher's Beach

I ALWAYS FIGURED THAT if you are on a beach near home, you might run into someone you know from work or school. And if that beach is a nudist beach, then one or both parties might be naked, so I didn't walk along my local beach in the height of summer as it might just be too awkward, depending on who I ran into, seeing as I'm a lecturer at the nearest college.

One day I was meandering around the local deserted sand dunes near, enjoying the early spring sun on a day when my workplace was closed.

From a distance, I saw a man stretched out, lazing horizontally in the long wild grass. He seemed lost in his own thoughts and didn't notice me wandering amid the tall beach heather with its pretty little pink and white flowers.

While I was some way off and still surrounded by the tall, thick vegetation, I realized he was stark naked. It wasn't surprising as it was a glorious day and an isolated spot.

He'd made himself comfortable with his legs spread wide apart. One forearm rested across his face, presumably shading his eyes from the bright sunlight. And his other hand gripped his dick. which pointed to the clear blue sky.

Fortunately. he hadn't noticed me coming, so I ducked behind a clump of towering sea oats and held my breath, hoping he wouldn't spot me hiding there.

When I peeked out, he'd let go of his impressive rod, and I had a clear view of his long, slender fingers running all over his body with a teasing gentle touch. It was like watching a master artist at work on a delicate canvas.

Having never seen someone caress themselves like that, I was completely entranced. I couldn't tear my eyes away.

I was glued to the spot, mesmerized, and taking in every delicious moment. It was the best entertainment I'd had in a long time, and I became a fascinated voyeur.

Now, I know it's shitty to spy on a guy having some private time, but it was a public place, and what was I supposed to do? It didn't seem right to go over and interrupt him or just walk past.

And anyway, it was the best original entertainment I'd had in a long while because I'd literally never seen anything like it in real life. My upbringing had been super-strict, and I'd never had a boyfriend. So, I was compelled to spy on him; I couldn't resist the temptation.

Even from a distance and half obscured by long grass, I could see the nude dude was fit, smokin' hot, as they say.

I imagined how it would feel to have a man's fingers stroke my skin like that. It must have felt good.

My body tingled all over as I watched him, taking his own entertainment in hand.

Sometimes his fingers dipped down between his thighs, and I couldn't see where they went or what they did there, but I could make a few guesses. Soon they reemerged, and his breathing got a little faster.

Did he stroke his taint or finger his butt while lying there and thinking he was all alone?

Would I like to see that?

I should leave.

I shouldn't have watched him.

Everything he did to himself, I imagined him doing the same to me and how it would feel. And I pictured myself doing those things to a fit naked man I found masturbating in a clearing in the forest.

His fingers caressing my chest while my hands held his cock. Touching him, caressing him, doing things with him. Things I'd never done before. Things that were sexual and obscene. And then doing them again.

I was so hot all over. I couldn't look away, and I couldn't move. I barely breathed.

Watching him aroused and doing things to himself, well, it got to me far more than it should. I was a pervy creeper, but I didn't stop looking; like turning away wasn't an option.

I pulled up my skirt and stroked my hand over my panties; they were soaked with my juices. My swollen clit protruded from its little place, making a bump in the flat fabric's surface, and it appreciated the contact when my palm moved over the nub.

My heart hammered fast and loud in my chest. Did he hear it beating? Did I make too much noise?

How far did the sound of the friction of my hands brushing over my clothing travel? Rubbing up and down over the top of my panties, giving some much-needed relief, but only some, not enough. The movements were more languid than my instincts urged because I imagined how he might do it – if he were to touch me as he did himself. He went slow, and it frustrated the hell out of me.

Fuck! Fuck! A slow hand and gentle would never be able to satisfy me. I needed a workman with big calloused hands to handle me rough, hard, and fast – it was my alone time goto fantasy.

While I watched, he didn't speed up the pace. The light-touch tickle and continuous edging seemed to make him perfectly happy. Like as if he had all the time in the world, so why not?

For me watching him was a perfectly glorious, protracted torture.

Doubts set in, and I wondered about moving further away to be at a safe distance — out of his range of sight and hearing — so that I could properly touch myself at my own pace and get the job done.

Soundlessly, I moved one foot and let my skirt fall back into place as I held my hands out to either side of me for balance.

Not a twig snapped. Not a single dried leaf rustled. I was queen of stealth.

Until the thinkable happened. As if sensing my presence, he turned his head, and his eyes locked on mine, freezing me in place like Medusa's gaze. He'd caught me red-handed and red-faced, spying on a naked Adonis.

To my surprise, he didn't react. He didn't jump up or try to cover himself. He didn't curse or chase me away. He just stared at me with a calm and knowing look in his eyes.

I stood there in complete shock, mouth agape, and feeling guilty as shit. As we locked eyes and I realized I knew exactly who he was.

I couldn't help but admire his confidence and composure. Who knew a guy caught naked and tugging his root in the woods would act so cool?

My mouth had gone sawdust dry, and I licked my lips.

"Do you want to come over here, Miss, and put that tongue to good use?" he asked.

"YOU KNEW I WAS HERE?" I don't know why I had to feel bad about it; he was the one who was wanking in public.

"Yeap," came his reply.

He obviously intended to shock me when he invited me to suck his cock, and he couldn't possibly really mean it as I was his college tutor.

If he knew I was there, did he care? Did he enjoy the danger and thrill of being caught? Was that performance intended for a voyeur's gaze? Did he know it was *me – his teacher from college* – watching and not some random stranger?

And two could play at his game. Never let the kids think they have one over on you, is one thing I learned in teacher training.

I wasn't going to be the one who backed down.

"And you're willing to risk my teeth, are you?"

"No teeth," he said. "Just that tongue and filthy mouth of yours will do fine."

My pussy throbbed at his brazen words because I was already turned on. I would never have allowed myself such fantasies about the man if I realized he was someone I knew and one of the students who I taught at the local university.

"I'm willing to give you pointers if you need to practice," Peter taunted.

Jeez! The dude had no sense of decency. And I want to hear more of his dirty talk.

But he had to be kidding and just talking shit because he was caught out, right?

Surely, he didn't actually want me – his teacher – to touch his cock!

But as he'd laid down the gauntlet, I wasn't going to back down. He'd have to be the one to call a halt. And he must've known that.

Slowly, I stepped towards him, giving him every chance to tell me to stop and admit he was only kidding.

But what if he didn't stop me? Perhaps he thought I was bluffing. How close would we get in this game of chicken?

HE WAS HORNY, AND SO was I.

My panties were soaked, and I was very aware of them each step closer as I approached.

He didn't stop me.

He continued to lay in the grass with his unfaltering erection waving at me.

I crouched beside him and admired close up his humongous dick with its smooth mushroom cap, meaty veined girth, and great length. Its magnificence made my mouth water. The dude was about ten years my junior and hung.

My God, so big.

No wonder he wanted to get it out and wave it about in public.

We were so close. If he didn't put a stop to this within the next few seconds, he'd be able to judge my cocksucking skills for himself.

I knew I shouldn't do it.

Not when we'd face each other again in class next term.

He might tell the world what I did and smear my reputation.

I've got this.

I KISSED THE BULBOUS head before parting my lips and pressing my tongue flat against the crown to taste him.

The oozing dew drops at the surface tasted of sweet bitterness, the flavor of a tradesman dipped in honey.

More.

I wanted more of his nectar, so I swirled my tongue around the crown, lapping up every droplet, and my student moaned.

Glancing up at his face, I recognized the look of intense arousal: his mouth was open, his eyes were closed, his breathing heavy. It seemed I was doing something right, and that encouraged me to continue.

Lowering my mouth over his dick, I let it enter me slowly until it stretched my lips to the limit, and I engulfed him. When his mega length filled my mouth and hit the back of my throat, there was still so much more to go. He was too big.

"Use your hand," he said as if what we were doing was perfectly normal, but his voice was gruff and shaky.

He reached over, took my left hand, and placed it at the base of his cock, so I wrapped my fingers around the part of his shaft that my lips didn't reach and squeezed.

With my other hand, I investigated his shaven balls, surprised by how soft they felt to the touch.

I gave his shaft a great going over, sucking and licking with enthusiasm; I wasn't going to let this boy think I was tricked into doing something I didn't want to do or thinking I was second-rate at anything. I was the older woman, and I had to show him I had skills.

This had better be the best blow job you've ever had.

Indeed he seemed impressed because it wasn't long before I tugged the juice right out of his ripe berries.

He groaned loudly. His hips lifted up off the ground.

I gripped his cock and pumped it while sucking furiously.

"Oh, yes. Don't stop."

I didn't need any encouragement because I rapidly discovered I loved sucking his cock. That wasn't a surprise to me. I loved sucking cocks.

I sucked harder and faster.

"Suck my cock. Suck it. Oh, fuck, that feels good."

That wasn't exactly helpful advice, but it encouraged me to continue and reassured me that I was doing it right for him.

The liquid explosion hit the back of my throat, and the thick, tangy liquor coated my mouth. I tried to catch every drop and swallow, but it was too much. It dribbled out of my mouth, onto my lips, and started to run down my chin.

I was on fire.

I wanted more. I needed more.

He'd opened my eyes and my mind to possibilities I never knew existed. And turned me on in a way I couldn't comprehend.

With my mouthful of his cream, I pulled away from him and sat upright.

He opened his eyes, looked at me, and blinked. Before he said anything, I opened my mouth to show him I was storing his cum in there and a little more escaped and dribbled down my chin.

"What the hell? I thought you'd swallowed it."

His expression was priceless.

He ran his hands through his hair, looking very much like a man who just been fucked.

I wish!

Yep, now I can say I've tasted you, I thought, though who the heck would I say it to?

He got his dick sucked, and I got a mouth full of cum.

Seems like a good deal?

I closed my mouth, swallowed, and wiped my chin with the back of my hand. He reached out and grabbed my wrist, pulling the same hand toward his face. Then he licked the remains of his semen from my skin.

The intimacy of it shocked me more than all that we'd done before.

My pussy flooded with juices, I was so incredibly turned on.

I wondered if I should pull away, but I had no life experience to draw on to help me navigate the situation. I didn't normally give blow jobs to guys I barely knew when I met them among the sand dunes, and never to guys I knew from the university.

I waited, expecting him to say something, but he didn't.

Instead, he moved his free hand to my thigh and ran his finger along the inside of my knee.

Then he did it again, and then a third time.

Each time, I felt an electric tingle that raced all the way to my toes in one direction and to my core in the other; it was a rush of excitement unlike anything I'd known before.

He kept running his finger further up my leg until he reached the hem of my skirt, which covered my pussy, and he didn't stop there. Instead, he slid his finger right up to the top and made the most erotic rumble somewhere deep in his chest when he discovered my panties were soaked, and so were the tops of my thighs.

I gasped and arched my back as he touched me.

I was still an untouched virgin, but I was ready for anything.

His fingers tickled and teased me in equal measure. He pushed my panties to one side and stroked along my slit. The sensation was the most amazing I'd ever experienced and leagues better than touching myself there.

When he reached it, he rolled my sensitive bud between his thumb and forefinger, making me writhe and moan.

His other hand suddenly went under my top and cupped my breast through my thin bra. He squeezed me hard, sending me crazy. He moved his fingers and twisted my nipples.

I squirmed on the grassy sand, unable to sit still. My hands flew up to cover my breasts with hard caresses of my own, but they weren't enough.

I tore at my shirt, desperate to get it off.

When I managed to rip it off, I flung it behind me, and I unhooked my bra; it also fell to the ground. Why not when he was already naked?

His eyes widened, but he didn't say a word.

We were past all words.

We were long past stopping because just perhaps students and tutors shouldn't do this.

Now it was time to see if he could make me come.

A smirk curved his lips. He shifted closer, and I leaned into him.

Our lips met, and his tongue flicked across mine, taking control of the kiss. Our tongues dueled with passion until I broke away from him and pushed him back on the grass.

He laughed. "I don't know if you're playing hard to get or you really want me."

"Neither," I said. "If this is a game, I won, and I think I deserve a prize."

"I dunno about any game. But do you wanna come sit on my face?"

He had no idea how much I wanted to do that!

I dropped down in front of him, straddling his lap.

"Then you're going to have to shuffle up here because my face isn't down there."

It made sense, I hadn't thought it through; I shuffled up his body and paused to check his reaction before I positioned my pussy directly over his mouth.

The look he gave my pussy was one I'll cherish: his eyes were wide and glazed with lust.

"Are you sure that's a good idea?" I asked, feeling self-conscious.

He was staring at my pussy as if it were the most beautiful thing in the world.

Young men your age aren't supposed to look at older women like that.

And teachers aren't supposed to do any of what I was doing.

But to hell with society, if I had a different job and he were any other lad, it would be okay.

I wanted him to enjoy what he saw.

My pussy was wet and swollen. It would take only a few strokes of his tongue to send me over the edge.

"Do you like my pussy?" I whispered.

He nodded. "You're so fucking wet."

His lips pressed against my lower lips, his warm breath washed over my overheated moist folds, then his tongue fluttered over my clit. I gasped and jerked forward.

His tongue continued to lap, circling my clit, and I couldn't believe the sensations rippling through me. My whole body clenched and released repeatedly.

"Yes. Yes. Do it. I'm close."

He sped up, swirling his tongue around my clit and sucking it into his mouth. Then he pushed his tongue inside me and wiggled it around before returning to my clit.

"Oh, God!" I screamed as I thrust, my juices gushing over his chin.

My climax both lasted forever and was over too quickly. When I was completely spent and collapsed on top of him.

"That was amazing," I mumbled.

"Yeah, well, I've had some good tutors."

"And I suppose you'll tell me next that you're an excellent student."

I lay there panting, wondering where my sudden confidence came from. I wasn't usually this bold or brazen. Yet I was certain I liked it.

I pulled myself off his chest and looked down at him. He stared up at me, and I knew he was thinking the same thing. We both liked it.

We were comfortable with each other in a way that probably wasn't right, but it felt right.

He moved and flipped me over onto my stomach. When he gripped my hips, he yanked me up, and I realized what he intended.

I was about to get fucked, well and truly fucked.

I WAS NERVOUS BUT EXCITED, and I suspected he must be too because he kept kissing my ass cheeks before moving his lips to the crack of my ass.

"You're such a naughty girl, aren't you?"

"Yes," I admitted. "I am."

He chuckled.

Then he buried his head between my legs and licked out my ass in a similar way to how he'd just been with my pussy.

I gasped. "Oh, wow. I didn't expect that."

So the game was on. In our competitive play to outdo the other with the shocking and unexpected, I'd suddenly lost my outright victory.

"How's that?" he asked when he surfaced to take a breath.

"Amazing." Unbelievably good.

He spread my cheeks apart and licked deeper making me wet back there while stimulating erotic nerve endings I didn't know existed.

"More? Please," I whimpered.

He slid a finger into my asshole and slowly pushed it in deeper. The sensation sent tremors through my body.

"Is this okay?"

"No, it's fine. It feels good."

"Good?" He chuckled. "This is the best part of the day."

"I feel like I've died and gone to heaven. Is that the answer you're looking for?"

"Better." He withdrew his finger, and I felt the much larger crown of his dick line up with my ass.

I bit my lip in anticipation.

"Well, you're about to become very familiar with this." He pressed his dick right into the crack but didn't penetrate it. "I think you are too tight there; we could work up to that next time."

Did he just say next time? When did we have that conversation?

Is there going to be a next time?

Then he lowered his dick, sliding it between my folds.

"Oh, fuck!" I cried.

"Fuck?" He repeated. "Do you want this inside you?"

I was still lying on my stomach, and he was above me. His cock banged against my pussy, teasing me, while he fingered my clit.

My student was about to fuck me. A man still in college. A man a whole decade younger than me. He wanted to do it, and I wanted it just as much.

"Yes. I want your cock."

Inside.

Me.

"Okay, then I'm gonna fuck your tight cunt and leave your ass until next time."

Next time!

It had taken me less than ten minutes to go from being scared of anal sex with this cheeky young devil to mentally begging him to put his prick in my ass. I guess that was his power of attraction.

Instead, he pushed his shaft inside my slippery wet hole with remarkable ease.

"You're so tight."

That can't have been true.

I was dripping wet with arousal.

So fucking good.

His fingers were strumming my clit, and pussy lips like a string instrument. And his dick carved its own route through my insides, hitting how many buttons of pleasure?

My head spun.

I panted and moaned.

"I love how you sound," he said. "I love hearing you scream."

Then he shifted position so his hips pressed against my ass, and he started pumping with the perfect fucking rhythm.

"You're so hot, babe," he growled.

I wriggled and shuddered.

"Does that feel good?"

"Yes."

"So fucking sexy. You're making me so fucking horny."

And then he got even more serious. He withdrew his cock and plunged back in harder than before.

"Oh, yes! Oh, yes!" I screamed.

"I can't hold on much longer."

He pounded my ass faster and harder.

"Tell me how it feels."

"Fucking great," I shouted. "I love it. Fuck me with your big cock."

He kept pounding me with renewed vigor; his skin slapped together noisily against mine.

"I'm coming, babe. I'm coming," he warned.

But the thought of a student filling me with his cum, plus the sensations that he delivered to me, sent me crashing over the edge.

I came violently, bucking against him with every last orgasmic spasm.

I heard him grunt and call out, "Miss! Miss!" as he came inside me.

I was spent. Totally and utterly exhausted, but somehow I found the strength to roll over and pull him on top of me.

"Thank you," I said.

"What for?"

"Pushing me into a new first-time experience. Sex among the sand dunes, I'll never forget it."

"First time? You haven't done any of this before? This isn't why you were prowling around here?"

I shook my head. "No."

"Wow, you're something special. You do know that people come here for this?" He shrugged as if it were common knowledge, and maybe it was but not to me.

Once it was over, I wondered whether he meant what he said about us doing it again. He didn't seem fazed by our encounter.

"What are we going to do?" I asked.

"Do?"

I nodded.

"What do you want to do?" he asked.

I shrugged. "Well, I don't want us to avoid each other and act strange because of this," I said. "But we can't tell people; you do know that, right? It's not like we can start dating or bragging or anything."

"Of course," he said. "What happens on the sand stays on the sand. It's the code; we only acknowledge this has happened when we're here. And if you want to do it again with me, I try to get here frequently when I can."

FOLLOW MAX GOO WHEREVER you follow your favourite authors to make sure you hear about future books.

You might also want to check out additional content on the Max Goo blog:

https://mrandmrsgoo.blogspot.com/

Watch out for more erotica shorts set in nudist environments.

All of the characters and places in my stories are entirely fictitious, though the stories might be loosely based on my real-life experiences.

Don't miss out!

Visit the website below and you can sign up to receive emails whenever Max Goo publishes a new book. There's no charge and no obligation.

https://books2read.com/r/B-A-HDZV-CVGDC

Connecting independent readers to independent writers.

Also by Max Goo

Nudist Adventures Collection
For My Valentine Erotica for Couples: Short Stories to Read Aloud in Bed

About the Author

Max loves reading and writing erotica, especially if it features curvy ladies and large groups of men. Her stories may be based on actual life experiences: She's confirming nothing. She's middle-aged and rebellious and lives in the UK with her brightly coloured hair.